Demise of a Devious Neighbor

A River's Edge Cozy Mystery

By

Elaine Orr

©2016 Annie Acorn Publishing LLC
Silver Spring, MD 20906
annieacornpublishing.com
@AAPublishingLLC

ISBN-13: 978-1542551403
ISBN-10: 1542551404

Cover Art by Angel Nichols
nicholsangel86@yahoo.com
http://www.angelwingsdesigner.com/bookcovers.htm

Disclaimer

Demise of a Devious Neighbor by Elaine Orr is a work of fiction. Any character resemblance to real people or events is completely accidental. A few literary liberties may have been taken when it comes to some geographic locations in the interest of creating great literature.

Dedication

In honor of all good pets who go before us.

Acknowledgments

Special thanks to the Decatur, Illinois critique group. Their good questions helped me see that what I think is obvious may not be. I also appreciate the several beta readers who take the time to read the book from beginning to end within a fairly short timeframe. I appreciate their enthusiasm. Copyeditor Lorena Shute does good work quickly, always appreciated. Finally, thanks to my sister Diane, who never misses an incongruity.

CHAPTER ONE

THE REVERBERATING BANGS SHOOK my nerves more than my truck, and Mister Tibbs would have wet the back seat of the pickup if I hadn't left the door open. She rocketed out just as the second Roman candle fizzled and headed toward the cornfield.

Either someone was aiming at my vehicle, or they didn't know fireworks were supposed to go upward.

I ended up on my tailbone on the hard dirt, hands splayed behind me. I stood slowly, searching the twilight for the source of the two salvos. Whoever had shot them off had surely meant to scare me. It worked.

The cicadas, silent for several seconds, rejoined the cawing starlings as they regrouped on the telephone wires. I whistled for Mister Tibbs and watched her crawl out from under a juniper tree next to my late parents' farmhouse.

I looked at her meekly wagging tail and stooped so she could walk into my arms. "I'd call you a super wuss, but I didn't like it either."

She licked my cheek and tried to aim herself for the back seat of the truck as I rose. If her multi-colored, short fur hadn't been mostly ringlets, the firecrackers would have curled it.

I lifted her onto her blanket, anxious to get back into the truck myself. After she circled twice and put her head on her paws, I raised my voice and yelled, "Whoever you are, you can't scare me."

No response, but the safety of the truck cab beckoned.

I got in, started the engine, and began to pull onto the gravel road, just as a sheriff's patrol car turned onto the lane from a nearby crossroad. I recognized Deputy Newt Harmon in the dusty cruiser and stayed put while he pulled into the driveway beside me.

We both lowered our windows, and I gestured toward the now vacant clapboard house. "I came out to eyeball the place, and someone shot off a couple roman candles."

Deputy Harmon is the youngest of the sheriff's staff, and his usually smooth brow wrinkled. "Hey, Melanie. Somebody was out here a couple nights ago, but closer to Peter Frost's place. They're shootin' off a lot more than sparklers."

I wanted to say I wouldn't have minded if they shot a firecracker at Frost, but instead said, "June's kind of early for fireworks lawbreakers. That why you're out here?"

"Partly." He grinned. "Had supper at my parents' place during my break."

I smiled back. "You're welcome to look around. Ambrose and I aren't going on the property until the lawsuit is settled, but legally it's still ours."

Almost as soon as my parents' funeral had ended, the farmer who owned the adjacent property came forth with the claim that my parents had planned to sell him their farm for a ridiculously low price. My brother and I were stunned.

Peter Frost claimed a verbal contract and had a piece of yellow-lined paper with a rough sketch of the property and a few words in my father's handwriting. Below the drawing, in Frost's handwriting, was a per-acre price that would have been believable fifteen years ago. Frost maintained that he and my parents had "begun to lay out the particulars," so he essentially had a verbal contract.

Bullshit.

The deputy shook his head. "Whoever did it's long gone. Not like we'd do footprint casts in a cornfield."

I nodded. "It's dry. As close as the corn is to the house, we're lucky they didn't start a fire."

In tandem we raised our windows against the humid June air of Southeast Iowa. Mister Tibbs said her goodbye from the back seat, paws on the side window.

After Harmon's cruiser drove back onto the road, I put the truck in reverse and did a two-point turn, so I faced the large yard. The thirty yards or so that separated the barn, on the left, from the house had seemed as large as a football field when I was young.

After my father sold the last milk cows, the barn had largely been used to store the tractor and other tools. At dusk, its shadow loomed over the yard, almost reaching the house.

The house. Each time I made a weekly check on the farm, I seethed. The house should not be vacant. I longed to see lights on in the kitchen and watch my father walk onto the side porch to stow his muddy boots before entering the house.

I usually only took a minute to go from sad to furious. I should be living in that farmhouse.

The breach-of-contract lawsuit Peter Frost lodged against my parents' estate, which meant against Ambrose and me, would wend through the court system, and our family lawyer had assured us that we would not be forced to sell the farm to him.

Next week would be a hearing before the Iowa District Court, and the dispute would be finished. Or the judge would rule in Frost's favor, and Ambrose and I would spend more money on legal fees. Or the judge would find in our favor, and Frost would appeal.

It was a mess.

In the meantime, we paid to have the property around the house mowed and contracted with two other farmers to plant and harvest corn and soybeans. Our lawyer had suggested we put any profit into an escrow account. That also ticked me off.

I could use some of that money. So could Ambrose. Instead of farming our land, which we would own outright, he rented land in Dubuque, near where his wife Sharon's family lived.

Movement near the barn caught my eye, and I squinted. In full daylight I could have discerned a human from a coyote or dog, but not near dusk.

Probably a coyote. The Donovans, who had the farm east of ours, said they'd seen one sitting on the cistern at the side of the house.

I put the truck in gear and backed onto the gravel road. Next week I'd make one of my reporter buddies drive out here with me. We'd bring a hunting rifle.

MY CELL PHONE RANG as I climbed the steps to my apartment. It's an attic, with a couple of dormers added, in Mrs. Keyser's house in River's Edge. I didn't recognize the number, but it was an Iowa area code, so I picked up.

"Melanie? It's Bruce Blackner here. I think I have something that belongs to you."

"If it's a winning lottery ticket, I'll split it with you."

He laughed. "No. A book or, rather, part of a book that apparently belonged to Hal Morris."

For a couple of seconds my brain dimmed. Hal Morris' murder hadn't exactly altered my life's trajectory. He'd already fired me from the *South County News,* and I'd just begun work as a gardener.

Along with the rest of the town, I didn't mourn him, but his death stunned me. For a few weeks, it had seemed as if life along the Des Moines River in Southeast Iowa was a lot less safe than anyone had thought.

"I don't think I ever lent Hal any books." I finished unlocking the door and placed my purse on a console table next to the entry door.

"Should've said it's a draft. Haven't read much of it, but your name is written in green marker on the first page, along with your cell number. I figured you were coauthoring something with him."

I glanced at my compact sitting room and laughed. "Hal hated how I wrote. Too terse for him. The only thing we ever did together was sign a couple of get-well cards."

"Huh."

"So, Bruce, where did you find this draft?"

"I should've said that first. You ever go on his boat? He kept it at Fairhaven."

Hal had kept a small, gas-powered cabin boat at the marina a few miles from River's Edge. "Nope. He never invited any *South County News* staff on a boat ride."

"Always heard he mostly kept it at the dock. Especially after he ran into the pilings that time."

I plopped on my couch and put one foot on the edge of the coffee table. My mother always said you shouldn't speak ill of the dead, but I had to make an exception for Hal. "I heard he was chewing out somebody for trying to pass him when he flooded his engine."

"No doubt. So, it's only a few chapters. If you don't want it, I guess I'll pitch it. Unless you know of family."

Hal had none. "Gee. Maybe I should take it. He could've talked to someone about it." I paused. "In fact, I think Shirley at the diner said Hal was writing a book or something."

"Good. I wasn't keen on pitching it, but I've got enough paper in the file cabinets."

"I'll stop by your office tomorrow."

"This could be right up your alley. Looks like a murder mystery."

FRIDAY MORNING Mister Tibbs and I had things to do before going to Blackner's Insurance. First on the agenda was running the vacuum in my two-bedroom apartment. A gardener tracks in a lot of dirt. I also changed out the older bedspread in the guest room for a fun yellow floral-patterned one I'd found at a rummage sale.

With that done, Mister Tibbs and I headed for Dr. Carver's house. She was my newest landscaping client. Mrs. Keyser recruited her, probably in part to be sure I could keep paying the rent.

I kept the cab window down, so I could smell air made fresh by last night's light showers. I love the smell, though our town of 7,500 never smells bad unless you drive by the alley behind Mason's Diner just before the dumpster's emptied. Or past one of the huge transports taking hogs to the meat packing plant just outside town.

I love River's Edge. Its town square provides a sense of cohesion that larger cities don't have. Several buildings on the square are empty at any given time, but the Chamber keeps the plate glass windows decorated with either displays about local history or ads for other businesses.

My apartment is on the north side of town on a block that once held beautiful Victorian homes. The remaining ones are past their glory days, and nearly all have been subdivided into apartments.

I'm fortunate to live in one of the smaller houses. It's a Sears bungalow, originally delivered via railroad, in pieces. The house has been converted to only two units and feels more like a private residence than an apartment.

My route to Dr. Carver's took me by the park at the edge of town, on the river, and I briefly glanced at the baseball diamonds. They had been spruced up for the upcoming July Fourth softball games, one of which pitted U.S. military vets against the combined memberships of the Lions and Rotary Clubs. It had to be a combination, since the vets in the clubs usually played on the military team.

At least rain wasn't expected again before the Fourth, here or upstream. The Des Moines River, which runs along the city park that houses the fields, would stay in its banks. Mud would not be the issue it had been the past two years.

I parked in Dr. Carver's driveway and studied the compact Cape Cod house. Most houses in River's Edge are at least fifty years old with frame construction. This house's brick structure meant it had been expensive to build. She paid a pretty penny to the former owner.

Two small evergreen trees, still in their burlap root balls, sat on either site of the walk that led to the screened-in front porch. Stooper and I had made the bushes his top priority. He said he would be on site earlier than usual, so he could plant them before the heat became stifling.

A horn beeped from the road, and I turned to see Stooper's beat-up Dodge Dart. At least, that's what it looked like. Rust was copious around the tires, and he'd replaced both back doors. Neither was the same color or matched the original blue, so I thought of his car as a rolling kaleidoscope.

Stooper couldn't pull into the narrow driveway without blocking me in, and he knew I didn't plan to stay. I backed out and pulled a few feet down the road to park. He entered the driveway, and Mister Tibbs and I walked toward him as Stooper got out of his car.

The walk gave me a chance to study the symmetry of what we were planning. Dr. Carver had said she wanted flowers and bushes equally distributed on both sides of her front walk. Yesterday, I had used a yardstick to be sure that the two azalea bushes we'd planted were directly across from each other.

Stooper raised a metal thermos of coffee to me, and I nodded. I'd always known his name, mostly because he had taken up his father's two professions – stone mason creator of headstones for the local cemetery and town drunk.

When I asked him to help me with a huge project at Syl Seaton's place, I thought it unlikely he could work more than a couple hours per day. He wasn't much older than my twenty-seven years, but his belly lapped over the waistband of his jeans and his perpetually red face spoke as much of high blood pressure as booze.

However, Stooper had apparently decided to reinvent himself through hauling soil and burning piles of brush. After just two months, he looked twenty-five pounds lighter and the Beer Rental Heaven Tavern had less revenue.

"Hey, Stooper. Looking good."

He twisted open the thermos top as he kicked his car door shut with one foot. "Getting there. Did you bring those gladiola bulbs?"

I snapped my fingers, which Mister Tibbs took as a reason to run around in circles and lick Stooper's hand.

"They're in the back of the truck. I'll grab them." I patted my thigh. "Come on, girl."

She cocked her head. Her plan had been to get Stooper to throw a ball for her.

"Okay, stay with Stooper. I'll be right back."

She ran around him twice before I'd gone three feet.

The back of my pickup was littered with gardening tools, an old quilt Mister Tibbs liked to snuggle with, a large bag of gladiolus bulbs, and two trays of marigolds and petunias.

I don't mind planting annuals, but it seems like such a waste of money to do more than a few in one yard. However, Dr. Carver wanted immediate color, so she would have it.

I took the bag of bulbs, lifted one tray of flowers, and started for the huge flowerbed that Stooper had created near the front of the house. The Scotch Pines would go on each side, the gladioli in the middle, and bedding plants around the edges.

Mister Tibbs barked, and I watched Stooper throw the now tooth-marked rubber ball at least fifty yards. Though he doesn't say so, I know it's to keep Mister Tibbs occupied so Stooper and I can talk for a minute.

"Hey, Mel. I should've offered to carry those."

I sat the bulbs and flat of flowers on the trunk of his car. "Stooper, you've seen me lift forty-pound bags of topsoil with one hand." I'm about five-six and sturdy. While no one would call me a pixie, I'm a good weight for my height.

He grinned. "Except when they break and the dirt spills out."

"Except for that. How's it going?"

"Not bad. I think Dr. Carver was kind of wary of me, 'cause she didn't know we were a team when she hired you. Pretty much got her charmed now."

"How did you win her over so quickly?"

"I helped her carry in a couple boxes of medical books and stuff when she made her last trip down from her old place."

Dr. Carver had been a partner in a busy internal medicine clinic in Sioux City. For some reason, she decided to move to the opposite end of the state, saying she wanted the tranquility of a Des Moines River town. She hadn't yet figured out it could be boisterous here, but if she went to the softball game she'd learn.

"A strong back wins them over every time."

He grabbed the tray of flowers and started for the flowerbed. "Heard people been setting off fireworks near your old place."

It's still my place. "Yep. Can't wait for the hearing next week, so we can get rid of Peter Frost and his claim on the farm once and for all."

"I hear you. What you up to today?"

"Couple things. Have to stop by the hardware store to pick up two trellises they ordered for Syl's place. And then, you won't believe this, Hal apparently left a partially finished novel on his boat."

Stooper stopped separating the marigolds and petunias. "Say what?"

"That's all I know. Bruce Blackner bought the boat and found it."

"Huh. You'da thought the auction people would've taken out all Hal's personal stuff."

I shrugged. "Guess Bruce bought it with the contents. I'm going to stop by his office."

Because she loves Dr. Carver's half-acre lot with its plethora of squirrels, it took five minutes to get Mister Tibbs' attention. She finally trotted up to me when Stooper called her. Very annoying.

After she settled on the back seat, I checked my phone for messages and turned to face her. "You know those squirrels will never let you catch them, right?"

Apparently she had run out her dog-o-meter, because she snored in low, even snuffles.

BLACKNER'S INSURANCE SAT just off the town square, not far from the *South County News*. Like most of downtown, such as it is, the company resides in a two-story, frame structure. It sits in the middle of a block-long strip of businesses.

While some buildings in town could use a lot of TLC, Blackner's place always has a fresh coat of paint. The deep burgundy canvas awning is fairly new, unlike others on the block.

The small insurance office lobby was empty so, as I shut the door, I called, "Melanie here, Bruce."

His voice came from down the hall, "Be there in a minute."

Mister Tibbs had heard my voice and yipped. I opened the door to the street and gave her a stern look. "No barking when you're tied to the post."

She seemed to get the message and settled into a spot in the shade, under the awning.

I shut the door and picked up a brochure about life insurance policies as lifetime annuities. I'd always been a saver, but not much since my parents' deaths. They'd had just enough insurance to cover the funerals. Ambrose and I figured that they had expected to leave us a nice inheritance with the farm. And they had.

A cough came from behind me. I hadn't heard Bruce approach from his office.

"Sorry. Compelling reading you have here." I placed the brochure back on the reception desk.

Blackner is in his early fifties and fit enough that no one would think him the grandfather of year-old twins. He smiled. "You aren't here for a sales pitch, but if you need investment advice let me know."

"Thanks to greedy Peter Frost, I have little beyond money for rent and my truck."

He grimaced. "Though I have no first-hand knowledge, I certainly never heard your father or mother talk about selling the farm to him. Or anybody else."

"No one did." I held my hand out for the manila folder he proffered. "Hal as author."

He let go of the folder. "Who would have thought? I always heard you or Fred corrected his typos."

"More like he never had the patience to write more than a few paragraphs at a time." I grinned. "Unless he insulted local insurance companies."

Bruce did an ungentlemanly snort, as he turned to go back to his office. "Let me know if it's a good read."

Mister Tibbs greeted me as if I'd been gone for three weeks, and I let her extend the leash its full twelve feet, so she could inspect the strip of grass in front of the local pharmacy.

As we walked to my truck, I glanced at the first page. Rather than open with Snoopy's dark-and-stormy-night phrase, the book began with, "It was well past twilight, and sleet was coming down in sheets."

"At least it's only one cliché," I murmured.

My mobile phone rang before I got to the end of the first paragraph, and I put the pages back into their manila folder. "Melanie here."

Through static I heard the clipped voice of Peter Frost. "Melanie. I'm calling to make a deal."

I said nothing for several seconds, and the static got worse.

"Did you hear me?"

"I did, but you need to talk to our lawyer. Ken Brownberg said that…"

"Bring him with you."

I wanted to tell Frost to shove it, but that would probably be counter-productive. "Um, to where?"

"Barn on your…" More static, and a couple of beeps.

"What? I can't hear you."

"Barn at your parents' old place. I'll be there at two-thirty." He either hung up or we lost the connection before I could tell him Ambrose and I owned the place.

I looked at the phone in my hand, willing it to ring again. Ken had told Ambrose and me not to contact Frost, but he hadn't said we couldn't talk if the old goat called us.

When my phone stayed silent, I pushed Ambrose's number.

He answered on the fifth ring. "Hey, you got my message."

"Nope. Telepathy."

"Smart ass. Just left it."

"Ah. I must've been on the phone with Peter Frost. You won't believe what he said."

"Called me, too. About twenty minutes ago. That's why I'm driving."

I realized the five rings were because he'd pulled over to answer the phone. Ambrose hates ear buds. "Did you talk to Ken about it?"

"You being in River's Edge, I thought you might grab him to meet us there."

I looked at my watch. It was eleven-thirty, and the drive from Dubuque to River's Edge would take three hours. "I'll call his office. What if he can't be there?"

"He has other lawyers in with him."

The sound of a truck's air horn came through the phone. "Sounds as if you should get driving."

"Yeah, not a big shoulder. See you at the barn. Maybe this'll all be over." As Ambrose hung up, I could almost see a big grin on his tanned face.

Over didn't seem likely. Frost would probably up his per-acre offer. We'd say no, and the hearing date would grow closer.

Or maybe Frost's lawyer had told him the so-called verbal agreement had no basis in reality, and Frost wanted to make an improved offer so he could still try to get it at less than market value.

Aloud, I said, "That won't work." At this stage, I wanted him smacked down and stuck with all the court costs and our legal bills.

I HEADED FOR the hardware store to pick up the trellises that Syl Seaton wanted me to use to tame rose bushes near his front fence. Setting them in his front yard would be the last major project at his property – for now, anyway.

Sandi had pointed me to Syl when I began doing gardening and landscaping work. He came in to place an ad for help on his five-acre property at the edge of town, and she told me about it before the ad ran. He became my first client.

Syl's good-looking, in a city sort of way. His easy good looks indicate a healthy bank account, and I've never seen him so much as perspire. The most casual clothes he wears are Dockers, never jeans.

I don't know what brought him from the Los Angeles area to southeastern Iowa, so I accept his change-of-pace explanation. I still don't get why he chose to live more than ninety miles from Des Moines, where he does most of his business. He works at home a fair bit, so I supposed the town he lived in didn't matter much.

I smiled to myself, thinking of his brown hair with its precise cut that says he got it at a salon rather than local barber. I like him. He has a wry sense of humor and doesn't look his age, which is early to mid-forties.

All four of the parking places in front of the hardware store were empty, so I didn't have to parallel park the truck precisely. It looked as if the displays in front were in transition from spring gardening to lawn mowing season. At least that's what the line of mowers and rakes made me think.

This early in the day, the air conditioning wasn't on, but a couple of box fans kept the air moving. The store sells everything from crock pots to Christmas decorations to chain saws. The proprietor, Jody, even maintains a bridal registry to encourage townspeople to shop locally.

Andy, the hardware store clerk, stood at his customary spot by the wooden checkout counter. He was also his usual annoying self. "So, Mel, anything new at Syl's place?"

Ever since I started landscaping work at Syl's property, Andy had seen it as his duty to raise the issue of whether Syl and I have more than a professional relationship. We don't.

I signed the account book that would let the store bill Syl directly. "Let's see. He got Stooper to replace the bottom slider on his barn door. The hostas your boss gave me have taken root really well. That's all I can think of."

Andy flushed. The gift of three plants had been owner Jody's way of apologizing for one of Andy's cracks. Not that he had to, but I appreciated the gesture.

"Stooper told me he fixed the barn."

I gave Andy my most brilliant smile. "Then you're up to date."

AFTER I ATE A LUNCH at home of potato salad and tomato soup, I took Mister Tibbs out to do her business. I planned to make Syl Seaton's my first stop after lunch, so I left her at the apartment.

Mister Tibbs has been to his place many times, and for some reason, she likes to dig in the flower beds. Probably because the soil is looser than in the rest of the yard. Apparently the squirrels had worn her out, because she offered no protest when I left.

Syl's driveway ends at the side door to his frame house, but his shiny green pickup truck was absent. That meant he had gone to Des Moines to work on his consulting contract with the insurance association. A glance around the front flower gardens told me I could wait another day before watering them thoroughly.

I wandered to the back of the house to check the few tomato and pepper plants I'd put in for him. Last night's brief showers had been just enough to keep them looking healthy.

A barn for hay and horses sits not far behind the house. Syl has no livestock of any kind, storing only a new riding mower and old tractor in the barn. He recently had it repainted red with white trim, which gives the acreage a kind of *Better Homes and Gardens* look.

I walked back to the front of the property, where I paced off good spots for the two trellises, next to the white front fence. They were to be centered, based on the house's position on the lot. It would take a while to train the roses to grow up instead of along the fence.

Stooper could use the post hole digger to help me put the trellises in place in the hard-packed soil. We'd have to either pour a lot of water to loosen it or wait until a soaking rain.

I glanced at my watch. Fifteen minutes before two, and my parents' farm was only ten minutes from Syl's. I didn't like to work in midday sun unless I had to, and I was already perspiring.

Though I knew where Syl hid a house key, I washed my face at the outside spigot and untied the scrunchie that had held my shoulder-length brown hair off my face. The short walk to my truck made me perspire again.

I had parked my aging green truck in a shady spot in the driveway. I'd sit in it and read part of Hal's masterpiece.

After automatically editing four pages of Hal's misspellings and laughing at the hero, whom Hal had clearly modeled on himself – intrepid newspaper publisher Harry Muldoon – I glanced at the dashboard clock.

"Oh, damn." I had less than five minutes to get to the farm. I threw the folder on the seat next to me and started the truck.

A quarter-mile from the farm, a siren sounded behind me. I pulled to the right. The speeding vehicle kicked up so much dust that it took a moment to discern whether it was a sheriff's car or an ambulance.

As the patrol cruiser sped past, the dust swirl parted enough to reveal Aaron Granger, Frost's nephew and my least favorite sheriff's deputy. Probably his uncle wanted him at the meeting, and Granger was late. The siren was overkill.

Had I known he'd be there, I would have said no dice, and Ambrose probably would have, too.

"Crud." I pulled back onto the road and made my way to the farm. Ambrose's car sat near the barn. Granger had pulled in behind him, leaving the cruiser door open.

Why would he be in such a hurry?

Raised male voices greeted me, and I half ran from the truck to the barn entrance.

Peter Frost lay sprawled on his back, motionless. Ambrose knelt next to him, holding a knife whose blade clearly had blood on it.

Aaron Granger was pointing a gun at my brother's chest.

CHAPTER TWO

WITHOUT THINKING, I yelled, "Granger, put the gun down!"

He swung partway toward me, gun still pointed in front of him. I ducked.

He turned back to Ambrose, his every word a bullet. "What the hell did you do, you bastard?"

When Granger's voice broke, it reinforced that a grief-stricken cop with a gun could be really dangerous.

I stood. "Aaron."

I'd rarely, if ever, used his first name, and he looked at me. I wasn't sure what shock looked like on a tall, muscled cop, but I thought I read it in his gray eyes.

"Your uncle called and asked us to meet him here."

Ambrose, still on the floor, raised his hands to shoulder height, to show he meant no threat to anyone. His right hand still held the knife. "I just got here. I found him."

My brother looked at Frost and back at Granger, tears now on Ambrose's cheeks. "I…it was automatic. I pulled the knife out. Maybe I shouldn't have. But…" He looked at the few drops of blood dripping on his shoulder and then at me.

I'd never seen an expression of helplessness on my big brother's face.

More softly than before, I said, "Aaron. I'm sorry about your uncle. Did you check for a pulse?"

Granger holstered his gun and spoke to Ambrose as he knelt. "Don't move, Perkins." He extended a hand to Peter Frost's neck.

The man had to be dead. No one could be that extraordinarily pale and have much blood in him. But where was all the blood?

Granger stood again and addressed Ambrose. "Put the knife down, and stand up slowly."

Ambrose did as instructed.

"Should I call an ambulance?" I asked.

Every bit of Granger's posture and movements said fury, but his grief and anger were morphing into professional deputy behavior. "I'll call." He motioned that Ambrose should stand near me.

He pulled from his belt an oversized mobile phone, which I recognized as some sort of law enforcement radio. "Need the coroner at the old Perkins' place." He paused, listening. "My Uncle Peter."

SHERIFF GALLAGHER stood to one side of the barn talking to Granger. Staff from the medical examiner's office and two firefighters loaded the body into the ME's van. In South County, the van usually transports people who die unexpectedly at home so the ME can determine cause of death.

Frost's was the second murder this year. Not good.

I used peripheral vision to glance at Ambrose. He's a lot taller than I am, almost six feet. His general demeanor is one of self-confidence, but even the tan he has from working in his fields didn't hide a pinched expression and decided pallor. I wondered if I looked as stressed.

Only a few cars had driven by, most of them other farmers. They waved at Ambrose or me. Until the official-looking van pulled in, they probably thought someone had broken into the barn. Not worth the time to stop if a farmer had work to do.

Now that the ME's van graced the property, a sheriff's deputy stood by the driveway entrance and motioned that cars should keep moving. Of course, each stopped to ask what was going on, which meant that word of Frost's death would be all over town in no time.

Gallagher clasped Granger briefly on the shoulder. He walked to Ambrose and me. "Melanie, Ambrose."

"Sheriff," we each said.

"I'll want to talk to you more at the office. Deputy Granger said you had a call from Frost saying to meet you here. Kind of odd, don't you think?"

I almost whispered, "The more I think about it, I'm not sure Frost was the person on the phone."

"What?" Ambrose asked.

"What do you mean?" Gallagher's tone was sharp.

"I heard a lot of noise on the line and…" I held up my phone. "It says caller unknown on my Caller ID."

I extended the phone, which showed the call, and handed it to Gallagher. "I know you can't tell for sure from this, but when you check the phone records and time, it'll help you see that."

He looked up from my phone. "I have your permission to get your records?"

I nodded, and Ambrose said, "Mine, too, of course." He looked at me. "There was static, but phone service out here is so spotty, I thought it was just static."

"Me, too." I hesitated. "Plus, it sounded different than regular static. Not as crackly."

"Crackly," Gallagher said. "Not a very specific description."

I frowned. "Kind of sounded like paper being crushed into a ball."

"You know," Ambrose said, "it kind of did."

Gallagher looked at us over his sunglasses, I thought sarcastically.

I pointed a finger at the sheriff. "I left a message for Ken Brownberg, asking him to meet us here. He didn't want us talking to Mr. Frost without him."

"So why did you?"

Ambrose gave more details on his call from Frost.

I nodded. "My call was almost word for word. I figured he wanted to up his lowball price just a bit, so the hearing didn't take place next week. But I can't say for sure Frost was on the phone. I wanted…anything that would make all the ugliness end."

"You know him well?" Gallagher asked.

Ambrose shrugged. "He bought his farm about, when?" He looked at me. "Eight, ten years ago? I was already at Iowa State."

"About then." I hesitated again. "To be honest, Mom and Dad never liked him much. He left his dog tied up outside even when it was super cold."

Gallagher nodded. "I'm the one who told him he had to get a dog house and put it so the wind would stay off the critter." He looked toward my truck. "Your mutt in there?"

I smiled for a second. "Worn out from chasing squirrels. She's home."

"Good. I didn't want him mucking up the crime scene." He rolled his eyes. "Yeah, I know it's a girl."

I had adopted Mister Tibbs not long after finding her in Syl's barn. Half the town knew her prior owner, now deceased, had named her Mister Tibbs because the woman had originally picked a boy from a litter. When the dogs were old enough to be adopted, someone else had taken the boy. The name stuck, even though Mister Tibbs was a girl puppy.

"I want you to ride back to town with me so we don't move your vehicles. I don't plan to impound them unless something jumps out at me, but if it's all right I may keep them overnight." He looked from Ambrose to me. "Assume it's okay if I look through them. Or maybe you want to talk to Brownberg first."

"I'm good," Ambrose said, and I nodded.

I didn't really like the idea. If someone had been trying to cast suspicion on either one of us, maybe they planted something.

Don't be so suspicious. Framing us didn't seem likely. Ambrose lived almost 180 miles away, and I'd been with my truck most of the day. Still, Ken wouldn't like us giving permission so blithely.

Gallagher turned to walk back to Granger. A vehicle honked from down the road, and the dust cloud turned out to be our lawyer's car.

"Speak of the devil," Ambrose said.

"I prefer to think of him as an ally," I said, dryly. "I called his office again when Gallagher talked to you."

Ken slammed the door of his black Lincoln and strode toward us. "I told you never to talk to Peter Frost without me!"

"You didn't get Mel's message?" Ambrose asked.

"Only just. I was driving down from Des Moines."

"And we didn't actually *talk* to him," I said.

"Not the point," he snapped and walked toward Gallagher.

I studied his back, always ramrod straight. He's maybe forty-five, and my parents' will designated him as the lawyer to manage their estate. He's always been an avuncular advisor. Now he seemed to be an annoyed attorney.

Ambrose turned to face me. "Anything you need to tell me?"

"Nope. I haven't seen Frost in maybe two months and then just at Hy-Vee, on the other side of the store. We never speak."

"I haven't talked to him since Mom and Dad's funeral. Or seen him, for that matter."

"You need to call Sharon?" I asked.

"Yeah. I'll do it from Gallagher's office and let him hear the conversation."

My sister-in-law is pretty unflappable. Still, hearing that Ambrose pulled a knife from a dead person, especially someone we all hated, from anyone other than Ambrose would likely upset her.

"Are we being too helpful?" I generally trusted Gallagher, but he definitely had to treat us as suspects, at least for a time. Hopefully a brief time.

"I dunno. We didn't do anything wrong."

"Gee, nobody ever gets accused of a crime they didn't commit."

Ambrose's raised eyebrows and frown were clear signs of irritation. "As soon as they figure out when the bastard died, they'll know we didn't do it."

"Maybe you, because you were on the road. And definitely don't call him a bastard when we're talking to Gallagher."

Ambrose grunted, almost half a laugh. "Weren't you in town?"

"Sure, but you watch detective shows. Somebody could say I had time to come out here and be back to my place for lunch."

Ken Brownberg spoke from just a few feet away and stopped in front of us. "Yes, they could. What in the hell made you two say Gallagher could look in your vehicles?"

"We didn't do..." Ambrose began.

"I know all about innocent until proven guilty," Brownberg said. "But until you can prove you are innocent, it doesn't count for much in the court of public opinion. Or in the sheriff's office."

"Jeez, Ken," Ambrose said.

"What do you want us to do?" I asked.

"If we tell him now that he can't look, it could seem that you're hiding something." He turned to walk to his car. "I have to stop by the office. I'll meet you at the law enforcement building."

Ambrose looked at me. "Probably not a good thing to piss off our lawyer."

AN HOUR LATER we had finished talking to Gallagher and Deputy Harmon. Newt had looked as nervous as a cat being stalked by a coyote.

I figured he probably hadn't worked on a murder investigation. Granger usually handled what would be called detective work in a larger department.

As Ambrose and I stood to leave, I asked, "When can we go back to the farm?"

Before the sheriff replied, Brownberg asked, "Why would you want to?"

"I check the place every week. I wonder if we should put some kind of security camera up or something. Probably be gawkers."

"Hadn't thought about that," Ambrose murmured.

Sheriff Gallagher stared at me. "I'll call you in a day or so. Soon as we're finished." He pointed a finger at me. "And *we* means *me*, Melanie. Keep your nose out of this."

"Yes sir."

The three of us left together, Ambrose and I to walk to my place.

Brownberg turned to me as he moved toward his car. "Don't answer any more questions without me, Melanie."

I started to protest, but he continued. "I'm not a criminal lawyer, you know that. If there is much beyond today, I'll give you two a recommendation." He walked away.

Ambrose and I watched him get into his car and then looked at each other.

I rubbed both temples briefly. "I don't get why he's so mad."

Ambrose turned in the direction of my apartment. "Bet he's mad at his office, too. They should've sent someone after you left that message for him."

I shrugged. "Maybe."

Before I could say more, the red Ford Focus that is the *South County News* staff car sped toward us. Its brakes squealed before Ryan threw it into park.

Sandi jumped out of the passenger side, her face almost as red as her hair, which frizzed because of the humidity. "What the hell, Mel? Why didn't you call us?"

"I figured you'd have been at the farm before we left."

"And the sheriff has our phones," Ambrose added. He eyed the car. "Is that yours?"

"We were over in Fairhaven. Somebody at Blackner's office told us about Hal's book."

I grinned. "You wanted to eat lunch at that soup and salad place."

"Sandi did." Ryan's deep blue eyes gave Ambrose an appraising look. "You need to borrow a car?"

"Since the sheriff has Mel's truck, it would save Sharon a trip to get me."

A town the size of River's Edge doesn't have a regular car rental place, though the Ford dealer will lend one if you're getting a repair. I didn't care about that now. "Let's go to my place. I'd rather talk there."

"Why does the sheriff have your cars?" Ryan asked.

"Can we explain at my place?" I asked.

"Good," Sandi said.

"I'll walk over to the paper and get mine for you," Ryan said. "Meet you there."

I watched his long legs stride toward the paper, which is housed in a one-story building just off the River's Edge town square.

At twenty-one, Ryan was savvy. He figured if he lent Ambrose his car for a day or so, Ambrose would talk to him anytime.

Ambrose got into the front seat of the Focus, and I rode in the back. I hid a smile as he tapped his fingers lightly on the door's armrest. He likes to be in the driver's seat.

Sandi's spoke in a clipped tone. "I can't believe Sheriff Gallagher didn't give you a ride."

"It's not like we're from out of town," Ambrose said.

"Except you are," she pointed out.

"Those are some well-honed reporting skills," I said. "You probably have some questions for Ambrose."

Ambrose chuckled, and his broad shoulders relaxed a bit.

"Same old Melanie." Sandi didn't smile. "Are you guys okay?"

"This time I didn't find the body," I said.

Ambrose turned toward the back seat. "Not funny. Even if it was Peter Frost."

"I know. I'm sorry you had to go through that."

Ambrose faced front again and glanced at his fingernails. Sheriff Gallagher's secretary, Sophie, had given him some special solution to get the blood off his hands.

"Ryan will kill me if I ask you a lot of questions before he's with us, but can you give me the gist?"

I gave her a thirty-second summary.

"That's so…weird."

I leaned forward. "The big question is who lured him there?"

"Lured?" Sandi asked.

Ambrose stared ahead. "Not our business."

"Did you notice the barn floor?" I asked.

"I squatted on it, remember?"

I softened my tone. "I know. I meant the dirt was flattened. Like there'd been heavy boxes on it. It should have had, I don't know, animal tracks, or a bunch of grass and brush that blew in."

Sandi said nothing, letting Ambrose process my question. When he didn't respond, she asked, "The barn has doors, right?"

"Yes. But old ones, and they're not air-tight." Ambrose turned his head to look at me. "I thought about that. It should've smelled like bird droppings, too. Wondered if Frost had stored stuff in there."

"Huh. I didn't think about that. Seems somebody would have seen him."

"Or seen anybody who shouldn't have been there," Sandi said.

"You can get in the back barn door directly from the cornfield," Ambrose reminded me.

Sandi turned into the driveway of Mrs. Keyser's house and we got out. I had hoped to get to the outside stairs on the side of the house that led to my apartment before my landlord spotted us. However, the sharp-eyed woman never misses anything.

The front door opened, and Mrs. Keyser came onto the porch. She's in her mid to late seventies and dresses on the least formal side of casual. She had on one of her brightly colored house dresses, this one with a rainbow, half on one side of the front snaps, half on the other.

"Melanie. What happened to poor Peter Frost?"

Under my breath, I said, "I knew she would've heard already."

Ambrose answered. "We sure don't know, ma'am. Very sad."

"I'll bet you'll hear something at the beauty shop," Sandi added.

"Good one," I whispered, then said. "Mr. Frost had already died when we got to our farm. We really don't know anything else."

We had continued to walk toward the back of this house and were almost out of Mrs. Keyser's line of vision. Unless she followed us. This could be a juicy enough story for her to do that.

"I have to walk Mister Tibbs later. I'll look for you."

She waved and walked back inside.

"You will?" Sandi asked.

"She says Mister Tibbs scares her cat. She won't talk long."

I HAD JUST taken a potty break and poured four glasses of iced tea when Ryan came tromping up the stairs. I let him in, and he glanced around quickly.

My two-bedroom apartment has a sloped roof. At about six feet tall, Ryan has to be careful where he stands.

He accepted the tea and downed it in one gulp. "Hot out there."

"It is. I'm brewing more. You can get yourself some ice water if you want something now."

He and I joined Sandi and Ambrose at my round kitchen table. It sits on the far side of the kitchen, which has windows on two sides. I just finished painting the window sills bright white. Before I sat, I lowered the beige window shades.

Mister Tibbs yipped from under the table, where she sat on Sandi's manicured toes. I wagged a finger at my pint-sized mutt. "Shhh."

Ryan pulled out a thin notebook. "So, where do we start?"

Ambrose frowned. "Whoa, Ryan. I know you have a story to write, but nobody's investigating anything here. That just gets Mel in trouble."

Sandi spoke before I did. "He just means start at the beginning, so we get the story right."

Ryan is definitely the more intense of my two former colleagues, partly because he's young and more because he wants to get noticed by a larger paper. While he would want to find facts himself, he also knew not to say that to Ambrose.

"Okay, I'll start." I outlined the phone call we had each received and how Ambrose had found Peter Frost just before Granger, and then I got to the barn.

"I just didn't think," Ambrose added. "I saw the knife in him…"

"Where?" Sandi asked.

Ambrose said, "In the barn."

It wasn't funny, but Sandi, Ryan, and I laughed.

Ambrose looked confused for a moment, then his expression cleared. "Oh. Kind of in his shoulder."

"Did it look as if he'd been in a fight? Black eye or anything?" Ryan asked.

As Ambrose relayed the lack of bruising or cuts, Sandi's mobile rang. She stood and walked to the living room. From the conversation, I could tell the caller was the *South County News's* temporary editor, Scott Holmes.

My chair faced Sandi as she stood in the kitchen doorway, speaking quietly. "Yes. We're interviewing Mel and her brother at her place." She stiffened and nodded. "Good point. Be there in a few."

Ryan and Ambrose looked at her as she came back to the table. She didn't sit. "Scott says that if we seem to be having a cozy chat, our reporting could seem biased."

Scott Holmes came to River's Edge as a favor to the chair of the newspaper's advisory board, Doc Shelton. Hal had been the sole owner, so the chain of command was not clear when he died.

No one except the staff and the board members knew the board's creation had been almost an apology for Hal's bombastic style. He took little advice. However, since no one had fought over the paper's assets, the district court judge dealing with Hal's estate allowed the board to make decisions and oversee finances, until the paper was sold in the probate process.

Doc Shelton, who has treated half the town at one time or another, is liked by everyone who meets him. He knew Holmes from the state Lions Club group, and Holmes had just retired as an assistant editor of an Iowa City paper.

Our temporary editor definitely had strong ideas about professionalism and avoiding the appearance of any conflict of interest. Very different from Hal, who often made a point by aiming a stapler at his staff.

Ambrose grinned and looked at Ryan. "Wait'll he hears you're lending me your car for a day or two."

"He'll be okay with that," Ryan said, and nodded to Ambrose. "It's not like you could hitch a ride to Dubuque on a hog truck."

Sandi picked up her purse. "We probably need to talk to the police more before we finish up with you guys." She grinned. "Plus, it'll give you two a better idea of what's going on."

Ryan stood. "One more question now. Why was Granger heading there?"

Ambrose and I just looked at each other. I suppose it was the shock of finding Peter Frost, but neither of us had thought to ask.

CHAPTER THREE

AT DUSK FRIDAY EVENING, I stood beside the huge garden Mrs. Keyser lets me plant in her back yard and watched Mister Tibbs sniff around the door to the shed where I keep my tools. Rabbits congregate in that spot because I throw half-dead plant stuff there so they'll eat less of the garden. Mister Tibbs gets frustrated at not finding bunnies where the scent is so strong.

It didn't seem likely that Ambrose would be charged with killing Peter Frost. I certainly didn't know much about how to assess when a person died. However, because Frost's head was its usual shape, rather than having drawn skin as it might have had after a day or so, it seemed likely he had died while Ambrose drove down from Dubuque.

Of course, I didn't know much about forensic science. Frost's paleness could have indicated that he had died a while ago. On the other hand, nothing smelled rancid.

I was more concerned about what had enticed him to come to our barn. After the Donovans told me they had seen his car by the house a couple of times, I talked to the county attorney, and he had told Frost to stay off our property.

If Frost saw a person in distress he might have pulled into the drive, but someone else should have seen something, too. County Road 270 had little traffic, and that meant residents noticed something unusual. Apparently, no one had.

I stooped to pull a few weeds around the tomato plants but quickly stood up. I hadn't seen Peter Frost's car or pickup at our barn. He could have walked over, of course, but on a warm day few people would walk the quarter-mile between his house and ours. I'd have to ask Sheriff Gallagher about Frost's car.

Mister Tibbs trotted over to deposit a short, thick stick at my feet. I picked it up and stopped mid-throw. The cylindrical shape reminded me of a roman candle. Could Frost have seen someone shooting off fireworks?

Mister Tibbs yipped, and I threw the stick as far as I could. She took off after it. In the early twilight of the late June evening, it took her several seconds to find it.

Briefly I thought about calling the sheriff to tell him about someone using the area near the house for the Fourth of July version of target practice. Surely Newt Harmon would have mentioned that.

Since personal use of fireworks other than sparklers and such is banned in Iowa, people tend to vary their lawbreaking locations. Since our house and barn were vacant, though, maybe not.

I put the thought aside. Frost was killed with a knife, not a projectile.

After pulling a few more weeds, I whistled to Mister Tibbs. She tilted her head, clearly not happy to see her leash in my hand. She let me attach it and followed meekly toward the front of the house.

She balked at going up the steps that led to the first-floor door Mrs. Keyser used to enter her house. In an unfortunate incident not long after Mrs. Keyser acquired her cat, Mister Tibbs had ended up with a deep scratch on her nose.

"Sissy." She cocked her head, and I tied the leash loosely around the bottom of the banister. The front of the house was closer to the street, so I didn't want her darting after a bird or squirrel.

Before I could walk up the steps, Mrs. Keyser opened her door and gestured to two white plastic chairs. "Why don't we sit out here, dear?"

"Sure." I glanced at Mister Tibbs. "Sit."

She obliged, panting slightly.

As I sat down next to her, Mrs. Keyser asked, "What more have you heard?"

I shook my head. "Not a thing. I'm not even sure where they took poor Mr. Frost's body."

She lowered her voice. "Did they find the gun?"

God love her. "I think he was killed with a knife, but I could be wrong."

She sighed. "I called Shirley at the diner, but she went to Ottumwa to shop today. Nobody knows anything."

That surprised me. The town grapevine is pretty strong. By now, someone should have talked about who last saw Peter Frost alive and when. At the very least there should be speculation about who was angry with him. Besides Ambrose and me.

"Pretty lonely out that way. Our farm sits between Frost and the Donovan farm, but there's that little rise. I don't think the Donovans could see from their house into the area around our barn."

"Drat." Mrs. Keyser tapped the arm of the chair with a bright orange fingernail. "Sure is humid out here."

I stood. "It is. Time for mosquitoes, too. I'll walk Mister Tibbs a few more minutes and then take her in."

"Now Melanie…"

I pulled a plastic grocery bag from the pocket of my jeans. "Pooper-picker-upper."

SATURDAY MORNING DIDN'T FEEL like a relaxing weekend day. After finishing a cup of coffee, I reached into my purse for my mobile phone to look up information on security cameras. I had three seconds of panic before remembering that Sheriff Gallagher still had it. "Nuts."

A two-minute search led me to the local yellow pages. I'd been using them in my bedroom to balance an uneven dresser that I'd inherited from my father's long-dead aunt.

The only security firm in River's Edge specialized in home security, so I called a company in Farmington that did systems for farms and outbuildings. The monthly cost of a monitored system was out of my ballpark.

I found some that would let me use my phone to see the barn and yard. But if I didn't watch, the place would be unmonitored. What would be the point?

I didn't need any additional expenses. Probably whoever had murdered Peter Frost would be too scared to come back.

I decided to assume that if there were local gawkers, all they would do was drive by. Or so I hoped.

A planned stop at the sheriff's office to get my phone meant Mister Tibbs should stay home. I settled her in the apartment and went back down to drive first to Dr. Carver's.

My parking space was empty. *Gee, no truck. How could you forget that?*

Because Mister Tibbs was not with me, I might be able to borrow Mrs. Keyser's car for a while. Assuming today wasn't one of her beauty shop or Canasta days.

Saturday morning Mrs. Keyser is not always up early, but it was eight o'clock and a light shone in her kitchen. I knocked.

She opened the door and smiled, broadly. "You forgot you didn't have your pickup, or you would've called Sandi for a ride."

Because she was so friendly, I didn't stare at the egg yolk on her house dress, which today was a river scene with fish jumping. "You're smarter than I am."

She dangled a car key on its chain. "I have a ten-thirty coffee catch-up with the gals from church, but you can use it until ten-fifteen."

"Thank you. I'm sure mine's ready, but you saved me a walk. Sandi or Ryan'll follow me back."

She frowned slightly. "Just make sure nobody else drives my car. I saw that Ryan screech around a corner near the diner last week."

I promised and thanked her again.

Since the sheriff might not be done with my truck, I planned to drop by the hardware store and Dr. Carver's first. I wanted to know what Andy had heard.

Me wanting to talk to Andy. Who knew?

I needed no excuse to shop, but since I had no reason to buy anything, I created one. I would get one of the natural solutions to spray on plants, so the deer didn't want to share my garden's bounty.

The front counter was vacant, so I walked toward the aisle with fertilizer, lawn seed, and such. It took a couple of minutes of label reading to decide on a product.

Deer-Be-Gone was meant to be mixed with water and sprayed on a plant. The all-natural product smelled like the worst kind of crud, so a deer would be crazy to eat leaves with it on them.

Andy stood at the wooden checkout counter when I walked to it. Half of a cinnamon donut sat on a napkin, and he hastily stowed it under the counter.

"You don't need to hide it on my account."

He wiped an apparently sugary hand on the canvas store apron he wore. "I didn't want to share."

I should have figured that.

I sat a crisp ten-dollar bill on the counter. "So, Andy, any big news around town?"

His eyes narrowed. "You usually don't fish for info. Course, you don't find a body every day." He cackled as he said "every day."

"It's a hard thing to see. *Most* people have been very sympathetic."

He rang up my order, seeming to have noted I didn't find him funny. "Alls I heard was that the sheriff don't know much." He handed me change. "Granger's pretty broke up. His uncle moved here to live near him."

I felt a pang of something. Not sympathy, but maybe close. In my head, Peter Frost was a demon with fangs. To Aaron Granger, he could have been the uncle who never missed sending a birthday present.

"I feel for him."

Andy's narrowed eyes said he didn't think I did.

The cash register is close to the front door, so as I turned to leave I almost bumped into two men coming in.

I knew the shorter one. Nelson McDonald graduated in my high school class – barely. He had been arrested a couple of times for receiving stolen property.

Each time he'd been able to convince the county attorney that he had responded to an ad on Craig's List and had no idea an item was stolen. It was a good con, because both times there had been an ad.

The person placing it used a bogus name and a Hotmail email address, so the ad couldn't be traced. That meant Nelson had an accomplice, because he wouldn't have been smart enough to plan that well.

"Hey, Nelson."

I started to brush past him, but he touched my arm. I tried not to stiffen, but did.

"You and Ambrose okay?"

I relaxed. "Yes. Good of you to ask." I looked at the second man, whom I didn't know.

"My cousin Harlan. He's visitin'."

I took in Harlan in an instant and didn't like what I saw. At almost six feet, he stood much taller than Nelson's five-eight. He also smelled like he smoked three packs a day, maybe mixed in with a little pot. It was his sullen expression that bothered me most.

"Ma'am," Harlan said, nodding a head of blond hair that most women would love to have.

"They know who done it?" Nelson asked.

I shook my head. "Not that I've heard. Sandi's all over it for the paper, so I bet there'll be a long story." When Nelson said nothing, I started through the door, which Harlan had kept open. "See you around."

I thought about Nelson and his cousin as I drove to Dr. Carver's. If I pumped gas next to him we'd say hello, but he didn't even talk to me when my parents died.

And how did he know Frost had been murdered? I reminded myself half the town probably knew within a few hours.

Just because my path crossed Nelson's and he asked me a question didn't mean he killed Frost or knew who did. I'd have to stop thinking like that when someone talked to me about Frost's death.

As I pulled into Dr. Carver's driveway, I admired how the front yard looked with half the petunias and marigolds planted. Usually I would have gone back in the late afternoon to help Stooper, if only to bring water. Yesterday I'd been too distracted.

Stooper was raking brush from underneath some shrubs. He took one hand off the rake and shook a finger at me.

I should have called him. I parked behind his car and walked to him.

"I have to hear from Shirley in the diner this morning that Peter Frost turned up dead in your barn?"

"Sorry, Stooper. All I could think about was Ambrose, and by evening I was pooped. I went to bed early."

I figured he would have been angrier if he'd read about it in the paper. The *South County News* only published three days a week, and today wasn't one of them.

I held out a jug of iced tea that I'd brought from the truck. "Peace offering?"

He picked up the cup that went with his thermos, threw out the old coffee, and held it out. I poured him a cupful of the cold tea.

"I'm not mad. I was worried. You and barns, it's not a good mix." He downed the tea and sat the cup on the ground.

"So far, my parents' barn has been safe for me." I smiled. "Thought I'd work awhile and then see if the sheriff'll tell me anything."

"Why don't you space out the marigolds and start planting those?"

I smiled to myself and knelt to do as he suggested. Technically, I'm in charge, but Stooper has become confident in his decisions. That's fine.

We worked in our usual comfortable silence. Stooper has never been a big talker. He worked with his grouchy father for years, learning the stone mason trade.

After his father died, as far as I knew, he'd worked alone on the small acreage a mile or so from Syl's place. In Stooper's case, acreage sort of meant dump.

Stooper had almost finished digging the hole for the second Scotch pine. He stopped and mopped his forehead with an old washcloth. "Heard Ambrose found him."

I set down my trowel. "It was horrible. Did you hear Ambrose pulled the knife out of Frost?"

"Jesus. No. Shirley didn't say that."

"Hmm. I wonder if the sheriff's people are more tight-lipped when it's one of their own? Frost was Granger's uncle." I placed a marigold plant in a hole.

"Forgot about that." Stooper stuck the spade deeper into the hole. "Granger's an ass-hole, but that don't make it right that his uncle got murdered."

I glanced at Stooper and then went on to the next spot for a marigold and stuck the trowel in the dirt. "You don't usually call people names."

"Him and me were in the same class. He called me lard ass a couple of times. Until I shoved him into a locker one day."

"Didn't know he was that mean. I mean, he's barely spoken to me since his uncle filed the lawsuit against Ambrose and me, but before that he was mostly just standoffish."

Stooper shrugged. "Gallagher tells the deputies if they treat people bad he'll hear about it. He probably taught Granger some manners."

I laughed. "I guess."

We worked for another half-hour in silence. Eventually, I stood and wiped dirt off my jeans. "I'm going to head down to talk to the sheriff and then stop by a few downtown businesses to see if we can plant the area near their curbs. If we got a few of those, they wouldn't need much maintenance."

"Who'd water 'em?" he asked.

"I think we'd charge them a small price to do the planting, and they'd water them. Maybe put in a couple of big pots. It would sort of be like advertising for us."

Us. Who would have thought I'd say 'us' about Stooper?

Stooper grinned. "You'll need a business name."

My keys were in my hand, and I'd started to walk to my truck. I turned. "Hadn't thought of it."

He smiled more broadly. "Want me to run a contest at the tavern?"

"Maybe the diner."

I KNEW SHERIFF GALLAGHER might not be in his office Saturday, but the murder apparently had him busy. His large frame was kind of squeezed into his desk chair.

He isn't so much fat as huge. He didn't look happy when Sophie ushered me in.

"Melanie, I pretty much told you I'd call you."

I sat in the wood chair opposite his large desk, which was piled with manila folders. "I know, but I need my phone and truck, plus I thought of a couple of things."

He handed me my phone, which had been sitting on his desk, and pulled a notepad and pencil toward him. "Go on."

"Did Newt tell you someone was firing Roman candles in the cornfield a couple of nights ago?"

Gallagher nodded. "Found some used tubes in the corn, not far back from the barn."

"Were any tire tracks near the barn's back door?"

He leaned across his desk and shook the pencil at me. "What makes you ask that? Who was using that barn?"

"So someone was? Ambrose and I didn't think it looked very abandoned. The floor looked..."

"You said it looked flat, like boxes had been on it. What kind of boxes?"

"How would we know? Ambrose hasn't even been down here for maybe a month."

"You go out there a lot."

I swallowed my irritation. "I sit in the driveway and eyeball the property. Ken Brownberg suggested we stay away until after the court rules. Rules in our favor."

He opened a manila folder. "What time did Ambrose leave Dubuque?"

I stared at the sheriff for a couple of seconds. Surely he didn't think Ambrose killed Peter Frost.

"He called me about eleven-thirty. I think he said he left home about twenty minutes before that, but since I wasn't thinking in terms of a murder investigation I didn't write it down. Do you need me to sign something for you to look at my phone records?"

"No, you gave it to me, so I scrolled through. If I need more, I'll get a warrant."

My cheeks flushed. "A warrant! That means you have strong suspicions."

His gaze was expressionless as he seemed to size me up. "It only takes a few seconds to kill."

I stood. "Ambrose would never stab someone. Never!"

His face was not expressionless now. He frowned and pointed to my chair. "Sit down, Melanie."

I wanted to walk out, but I wanted information more. I sat.

"You were a reporter. You know it's the facts that matter. Fact is, Ambrose was holding the weapon that killed Peter Frost. Peter Frost who filed a lawsuit to get your parents' farm for next to nothing."

I seethed, but tried not to show it. "True. But Ambrose doesn't even like to hunt. He wouldn't kill anyone."

"Fury can be a big motivator." At my angry look he held up a hand, palm facing me. "I like Ambrose. And you, when you aren't interfering. Only an idiot would ignore Ambrose, and I'm no idiot."

He had a point. I swallowed my anger. "I don't think you are. Do you know what was kept in the barn?"

Gallagher shook his head. "No idea, if anything. For all we know, a neighbor kept bales of hay in there over winter."

"No tiny bits of hay on the floor."

"Ever hear of a broom?"

"Besides," I persisted, "no one told us anyone spent time on the farm, much less used the barn."

He nodded. "Except for the time you asked County Attorney Smith to keep Frost off the property."

I nodded. "Mr. and Mrs. Donovan saw him there."

"We've talked to everyone up and down County Road 270. But if someone stayed alert, no one would see them."

I had to agree. Both Donovans worked their fields, meaning they were out of their house most days. If Peter Frost had noticed something, he'd never tell.

To try a different tack in my search for information, I asked, "Do you know what time Mr. Frost died?"

"I've learned never to guess. I'm waiting for the ME's report."

I made a mental note to see if Dr. MacGregor at the hospital would talk to me when he finished the report.

"How come Granger drove like a bat out of hell to get there? Ambrose didn't have time to call."

Gallagher didn't respond at first, but seemed to decide he could. "Deputy Granger had a call from his uncle. He just missed the call, and it went to his voice mail."

"So why speed?"

Gallagher raised his eyebrows, as if he thought my question impertinent or something. "He thought Frost sounded upset, and then when Granger called back he didn't answer."

"The message must've said something about his uncle being at our place, or Granger would have gone..."

"Leave it alone, Melanie."

I stared at Gallagher and drew a breath. "I didn't see Peter Frost's car on our property."

Gallagher's tone invited no more questions on that topic. "Neither did I."

"What about who called Ambrose and me? Can't you, I don't know, get our mobile phone company to tell you who called us?"

"Would make my job easier. I made a request to the local cell people, but anyone can block their name. My bet is it's one of those monthly phones. All it will show is the location of the call. Not relevant anyway."

"Why...?" I began.

"Because I figure Doc MacGregor's report will show that Frost died about when Ambrose got to the barn."

Gallagher began to stand, but his phone rang and he sat back down. As he did, he pointed toward the door.

I'd been dismissed. I hadn't reached the door when Gallagher sat up straighter and began writing rapidly on his pad.

THE BETWEEN BREAKFAST AND LUNCH crowd at Mason's Diner is small, especially on a Saturday. I wasn't meeting anyone. I only wanted to hear what Shirley knew. Especially because she was out of town yesterday, her news antennae would be high today.

The diner is a River's Edge institution and looks like any diner from 1950s TV shows. It's the basic shape of a thick cigar, but booths with red plastic seating also run down one side, making it an L shape.

The counter's rotating stools would be higher if they were made today. Spinning on those stools is as popular for six-year olds now as it was for me and my friends.

Shirley stood behind the counter, taking an order from a woman on a stool. Given the customer's practical shoes, worn with a dark blue tee-shirt and jeans, I thought she was probably a farmer in town on an errand. I didn't recognize her, but I didn't know quite everyone.

I slid into my usual booth in the back and glanced out the window. The sun pounded the asphalt, but as I looked it moved behind a cloud.

The diner is just off the square. Today, the street of two-story buildings in varied colors and conditions looked almost serene. On such a clear day, how could anyone suspect my brother of murder?

Shirley appeared next to my booth, tapping her pad with a stubby pencil. "How come Peter Frost went to your barn?"

"Hello to you, too."

Her smile was quick and impish under an almost beehive hairdo. "You know I don't like to waste time. Could be another customer in here any minute."

I gave her half a smile. "No one seems to know. Had you heard any talk about people shooting off fireworks at my parents' old place?"

She frowned. "Seems to be a lot more around town than usual this year."

"Hmm. You know how close the Missouri border is. Think someone's bringing more across the border this year?"

Shirley's quick shrug implied impatience. "Haven't heard anything."

I glanced at the six older people spread around the diner. "I don't think this is the crowd to tell you about it."

She followed my gaze. "What do you think fireworks have to do with it?"

"Probably nothing. It's just the only thing different out there."

"As far as you know." The front door opened, and Shirley looked at it and lowered her voice. "Mrs. Waters doesn't like waiting even five seconds. You keep thinking."

She hadn't asked for my order, but I knew Shirley would bring me hot tea and half a bagel in a few minutes. Usually she dishes information as soon as she sees someone, so she clearly knew nothing.

I pulled a notepad from my purse and started to make a list of business owners to talk to, who might want a planter in front of their store or office. I was concentrating so hard I didn't notice Sandi until she slid into the booth across from me.

"Mel. I didn't want you to hear this from anyone else."

"What? Is Ryan okay?"

"Yes." She leaned across the table and spoke so low I could hardly hear her. "I got a call from someone at the hospital. Based on his body's temperature, Peter Frost probably died about the time you guys got to the barn."

Her green eyes started to redden. "Ambrose would have had time to kill him."

CHAPTER FOUR

I WOULD HAVE JUMPED up, but Shirley had arrived at the booth with my hot tea and bagel. I didn't want her to grill me.

"Okay, sugar, now you know something." She set the mug down hard enough to make the tea slop over the edge.

Sandi hissed. "Quiet, Shirley."

Shirley adjusted her mustard-color uniform skirt. "Okay, so *you* know. That's better."

I stayed seated. "But she can't compromise a source."

"That's big city talk." Shirley stared at Sandi. "How often do you and your buddy ask me what's going on?"

Sandi shut her eyes briefly. "Okay, the ME has some findings. You usually get that before I do. Why don't you call and ask? If you can't find out, I'll tell you."

Shirley cracked her gum as she walked away. "Fair enough. Eat that bagel before it's cold."

I met Sandi's gaze. "Someone else could've just left."

"Gallagher won't be rash. But you two were furious with Frost."

I loosened my scrunchie and shook my head of brown hair for a few seconds before refastening the ponytail.

"Getting the rocks rattled?" Sandi asked.

I spread jelly on my bagel. "I should call Ambrose."

She frowned. "Okay, but if he gets a call from the sheriff, make sure he doesn't let on that he knows. Gallagher'd figure out in a heartbeat that I told you."

"Why?"

"You know Rosemary at the front desk in the ME's office? I dated her brother in high school. She said the rectal thermometer used at the barn," Sandi made a face, "registered almost exactly 98.6 degrees."

I rolled my eyes and glanced around the diner to make sure no one could hear us, then dialed, thinking as I did.

On crime shows, one way to tell time of death before autopsy was simply to compare a body's temperature to the ambient air temperature. Frost's body was more like a living person's temperature than the eighty-two degrees of the day he died.

Ambrose's home phone rang six times and went to voice mail. He likely had work in the fields. "Hey, Ambrose. Not sure if it means anything, but we've heard Frost died not too long before we got there."

"Tell him," Sandi said.

"And Sandi said not to let on that you know that, because she isn't supposed to know. Don't worry about it. Call me." I pushed the end button.

"He'll tell."

I had to smile. "He won't. Besides, in an hour a lot of people will know."

She shook her head. "Not much coming out of the sheriff's office on this one."

"Hey, speaking of them. I checked when I was leaving Gallagher's office, and I can get my truck. Would you...?"

"You didn't tell me you went there!"

"Excuse me, you just walked in."

Shirley called from the counter as she cleared away used coffee cups. "Found out. Thanks, Sugar."

Sandi turned, waved to her, and then looked back at me. "What did he say?"

"Only one thing that mattered much." I told her about Granger getting the call from his uncle. "But either Frost didn't say much, or Gallagher isn't saying."

Sandi took a pen and small pad from her purse.

"Timeline?" I asked.

She nodded. After putting our heads together, literally so no one would listen, we started a list.

1. Ambrose gets call from someone saying they're Frost. Maybe 11.
2. Ambrose leaves Dubuque. About 11:20
3. Melanie gets call from Frost or someone. About 11:40
4. Where was Frost during this time?
5. Mel goes to hardware store. About 11:45
6. Mel goes to Syl's, reads Hal's book. About 12:10

"Hal's book? It's readable?"

I shrugged. "I didn't say it would get published, but the words string together."

"Later," Sandi said, and we kept going.

7. Mel drives to farm. 2:25
8. Granger passes her. 2:35
9. Ambrose and Granger in the barn with Frost. About 2:40
10. Mel gets there, about same time.
11. ME, sheriff, Brownberg at farm. 3:00 – 4:00
12. Sheriff keeps M and A's vehicles. 4:00-ish

We were diverted by Sandi wishing she and Ryan hadn't gone to Fairhaven to look for information on Hal's boat.

"Spilt milk," I said. "Keep going."

13. Questioning at sheriff's. No Granger there. 4:00 – 5:00
14. Sheriff warns Mel to leave alone. Always

We stopped and looked at each other.

"We could go on," Sandi said, "but this is what matters. In fact, it's the part leading up to Ambrose finding him that matters most. That's what we know nothing about."

I pointed at the list. "We need to see the medical examiner's report."

"Why? We know when he died."

"Yes, but what if the killer stabbed him earlier? How long would it take someone to die?"

Sandi squinted and wrinkled her nose. "That's an awful thought."

"It's eventually made public, but that could be a while." My mobile buzzed, and I looked at it and back at Sandi. "Ambrose."

"What, Mel? How long before?"

"Don't know. We only heard that and haven't seen the full ME report."

"What's an ME...oh. Right. Get out of there!"

The sound of a braying goat told me what annoyed Ambrose. He raises a few goats and gives most of their milk to some group that provides it to families with kids who are allergic to cow's milk.

"Ambrose?"

Sandi had heard the goat and giggled.

He came back on the phone. "Keeps trying to eat Sharon's begonias and the recycling bin. Well, they can't pinpoint within minutes, can they?"

"I wouldn't think so. I hoped it would show he'd been dead a few hours or something."

Sandi nodded.

Ambrose sighed. "What do we do?"

"Find out when we can go back to the farm and look around the barn."

"Melanie!"

"I'll ask the sheriff. And I'll take Ryan or Stooper."

Sandi sat up straighter. "Hey."

"Like you'd be good in a fight," I said.

"Damn it, Mel."

I could hear the frustration in Ambrose's voice, and smiled. "I promise I won't go until the sheriff says I can. Won't be much to see, but who besides us would spot something odd?"

From the phone came, "Ow! Get the hell away from me!"

I laughed. "What did it do?"

"Head-butted my knee. Gotta go. Behave yourself."

He hung up, and I looked at Sandi. "We need to go back to the sheriff's office anyway." I looked at the time on my phone. "Damn. I need to get Mrs. Keyser's car back by ten-fifteen."

"Car? Oh, you need me to drive your truck back from the sheriff's?"

I put some money on the table. "That would be great, and then I'll drop you back at your car."

I stood as Shirley neared us with a cup of coffee for Sandi. I nodded at Shirley. "Put it in a to-go cup for her, and I'll get it."

I added two dollars to the amount on the table. "I have to get my truck at the sheriff's and take Mrs. Keyser hers."

"Oh, sure. She'll be in here at ten-thirty."

Sandi looked amused as she regarded Shirley's back. "So nice our lives in this town are private."

MISTER TIBBS RACED around the two raised beds that held my large vegetable garden in Mrs. Keyser's back yard. After several nights, I had figured out that the mid-sized rabbit was leading a race and would never allow itself to be captured. Mister Tibbs hadn't caught on yet.

From my kneeling position, I dug the metal weeder into a huge dandelion that had wedged itself between two tomato plants. It felt good to take out my frustrations on inanimate objects.

I sat back on my heels. The motion had reminded me of stabbing something. "Ugh."

I stood, surveying the bounty of vegetables. Summer had come early, so I had enough tomatoes and peppers to share space at the farmers' market Sunday.

Generally the other co-op members only let regulars share the tables, but I'd kept up my dues for years and rarely sold, so they let me in. I wouldn't earn much money. I usually went for the company of other growers. This weekend I wanted to see if anyone knew more about strangers at our farm.

I bent down again and pulled the dandelion's six-inch root. "Big sucker, aren't you?"

I surveyed the bed next to the one I was weeding. It got less sun, and the squash plants were undersized for the first of July. I'd aerate the soil around them more and, perhaps, put down some different fertilizer.

A worn-out Mister Tibbs came back and plopped onto a cool spot of dirt, panting.

"I didn't bring out water for you. We'll go inside in a minute. We have to pick stuff tomorrow and get to the market." I didn't add that she wouldn't accompany me. I'd make sure she wore herself out while I loaded bushel baskets and put them in the pickup.

My plan had been to pick vegetables and basically distract myself in the peace of the garden. Didn't work. Mister Tibbs put her head on my ankle-high boot and looked up.

"Sorry. I'm not in much of a mood to play." She cocked her head and raised one pointed ear, so I bent to scratch her head.

"Why would anyone want to make it look as if Ambrose or I killed Peter Frost? I halfway get why anyone would want him dead, but why in our barn?"

She yawned, and I gently pulled my boot from under her head. "Come on. Time to put stuff away."

I walked around the raised beds one more time, picking up the trowel, weeder, and fairly new hoe. To keep Mister Tibbs out of the shed where I store tools and fertilizer, I gently raised my left foot in her direction. "No smelling the fertilizer."

CHAPTER FIVE

SUNDAY MORNING, I SKIPPED the Methodist service in favor of coffee with Sandi at the diner. The *South County News* article scheduled for Monday, which Sandi had emailed me, didn't have any information I didn't already know.

She'd call me if she found something important, but I wanted to know anything she knew. I might see relevance in something she thought immaterial.

By nine-thirty, I assumed Sandi had forgotten or was still with her Saturday night date, whoever that had been. Sandi and I don't talk a lot about our love lives, not that I had much of one at the moment. She was devastated when her last relationship ended abruptly, even if she doesn't say much. Still, I try to be empathetic.

I put the tip on the table and began to stand just as she walked in, breathless.

Sandi nodded at me, then waved at the often-bumbling Sunday waiter and pointed at me. He would likely remember that she wanted tomato juice and oatmeal, a combination that made me want to retch.

"Hey, Sandi."

She slid into the booth across from me, grinning broadly. "I know where Peter Frost spent part of Friday morning."

"Do tell."

"He drove to Fairhaven to see about renting a boat slip."

If Sandi had told me he went to hell to make a reservation, I might have been less surprised. "You can see into his barns. There's no boat."

"I asked a few people. He may never have even been on one."

"No reason to," I mused. "I don't suppose he asked to rent Hal's space."

Sandi shook her head. "Bruce Blackner still has Hal's old boat in it. But Frost did ask if he could see Hal's boat. The guy who rents the slips told Frost it had been sold, so no dice."

My mind churned. Bruce told me about the manuscript on Thursday. He might not have told anyone else, but if he as much as mentioned it at the diner or told even one person, word that Hal was writing a book would be all over town. The fact that it was on Hal's boat when Bruce bought it, a place Hal didn't go often, would have added to the speed of the gossip chain.

"Melanie."

"Sorry. I was thinking. If he didn't really want a boat, he might have been looking for the manuscript."

"I agree. What the heck is in it?"

A few days ago that manuscript had seemed, if not important, funny. Now I couldn't even remember where I had put the damn thing. Had to be in my truck. "I only read the first four pages."

Sandi leaned back in the booth so the server could put her oatmeal on the table. When he walked away, she looked at me. "Was it long?"

I shrugged. "No, maybe forty pages. I'll go out to the truck and get it." I left her blowing on her hot oatmeal as I walked away.

After five hot minutes of looking under the seats, in the glove box, and under the floor mats, I gave up. I hadn't taken the manuscript into my apartment. That meant someone had taken it. What would Hal have written that was worth stealing?

Sandi looked at my scowl as I slid into the booth. "You didn't find it?"

"I think someone took it." I said this before I thought to remind Sandi not to screech. It's her worst habit.

Sandi reddened and gave a short wave to the waiter, letting him know her squeal didn't indicate a bug in her food or something, then turned back to me. "Did you lend it to Ambrose?"

I shook my head. "No. It was on the front seat of the truck when we found Peter Frost. Then the sheriff had the truck. I need to get that manuscript."

"So, go get it."

"It's Sunday. Gallagher won't be there, and I don't want to make a fuss with anyone else."

Sandi raised an eyebrow at that. "You aren't acting like you used to be a newspaper reporter."

"Yes, I am. If Gallagher has it in some kind of property storage, he'll just give it to me. He probably forgot. If I ask someone else, it'll be all over town that I'm looking for it."

I glanced at my watch. "I picked most of my vegetables already, but I need to swing by to load the pickup and get to the market."

"But you'll share with me, right?"

I grinned. "Don't I always?"

Sandi paused with her glass of tomato juice halfway to her lips. "When it's convenient for you."

THE SUNDAY AFTERNOON FARMER'S MARKET IN River's Edge is the only one in the county held then. It's probably the only one in any Iowa county, for that matter. Our farmers picked that time because there's no competition. It can't be Sunday morning, of course, since half the town goes to church.

I sat at the table I shared with Sam Harris and glanced around the market, which is in the parking lot of a small strip mall on the outskirts of town. There aren't usually more than fifteen or twenty tables, but most farmers bring a lot of plants or vegetables. Not too many fruit growers, except for all the strawberries and rhubarb in early spring and apples in late summer.

A couple, with twin girls who looked to be about two, selected sweet corn from the vendor at the table across from me. I didn't recognize them, but the market attracted people from neighboring counties, so I never knew everyone.

"You don't have any tomatoes?" The woman asked the guy.

I called to her. "Mine are really good." I smiled as she turned to face me.

The farmer she had been talking to was an old friend of my Dad's, and he winked at me as she walked over.

"My name's Melanie. Are you from South County?"

She returned my smile. "We drove down from Iowa City. It's so peaceful here."

The husband, who had stooped to look at the girls in the stroller, added, "And it's really fun to drive seventy miles with two chatterboxes."

They were both about thirty and fit. I marked them as graduate students or young assistant professors at the University of Iowa.

I nodded at the twins. "You two have more guts than I do." I gestured at the neatly arrayed tomatoes in front of me. "I picked these last night. I have a large garden behind the house."

I had almost said behind my house, but thanks to the late Peter Frost, I didn't have a house. Maybe I would again soon.

I sold them four tomatoes, and Sam convinced the twins' Dad that Sam's sweet onions were the best in the market.

When they had moved on, I turned to Sam. "Have you been to all the markets this year?"

"All but one. My son's birthday was two weekends ago."

We talked about his son's party in between customers, and when our pauses were longer than half a minute, Sam said, "I'm sorry about old Frost being found at your place."

I looked at him directly and then at shoppers at a table diagonal from us. "You don't know the half of it. Really awful. Especially for Ambrose."

"Yeah, I heard at the gas station that he found the guy."

Nothing in Sam's tone implied that he thought Ambrose killed Frost, so I didn't change the subject. "I know you don't live near our farm, but had you heard Frost was going to our barn sometimes?"

"Nope, but no reason for anyone to talk to me about his comings and goings." He glanced around and, seeing no one near us, continued. "I heard guys at the diner saying he owed the grain elevator a good bit of money."

Loads of raw corn aren't good for much except feeding hogs. The South County Elevator is also a grist mill. It processes corn and stores the resulting grain in its huge silos until it's bought.

A lot of farmers would pay the grain elevator even before buying propane to heat their houses. Certainly before shoes for the kids.

"Huh. Guess I don't know much about him. I assumed that, since he bought that farm when he was, well, old, that he had assets."

"Like I say, I didn't know him except to say hey. Just what I heard."

"Did you hear anything at all about anyone using our barn?"

"Using it? No. I thought your farm was tied up in some kind of estate deal."

"It has been. I don't know exactly what will happen now."

For the next twenty minutes we bantered with local people out to get their weekly vegetables. We also explained to town people from Fairfield or Keokuk things like the difference between the vine tomatoes they saw in grocery stores and truly fresh tomatoes.

In even the recent past, whether you grew up in a town or on a farm, you'd have known a lot about farming. Not so now that there were fewer small farms and more big operations. Hardly any town kids had nearby relatives with farms to visit.

Foot traffic slowed, so I turned to Sam. "I need some good organic fertilizer. I bought the last batch at the hardware store, and I'm not sure it did the trick."

Sam graduated two years behind me in high school, but even upperclassmen knew him as the best practical joker in the school. I wouldn't sit in any chair he held out for me without looking first, but he gives top-notch advice on growing vegetables.

"I pretty much make my own from our milk cows." He glanced around the twenty or so tables, until his eyes fell on two guys who were in their mid-thirties, roughly Ambrose's age.

Like Sam, they hadn't gone away to college, though I knew they had taken some classes at Iowa State and were active in the County Extension Service.

Sam nodded at the two men, who I thought were named Brad Thomas and David Bates. "Brad and David have some pretty good stuff. You pay them in here, and then they load from their truck to your pickup on the far side of the parking lot."

That suited me fine so I walked over to their table. The only produce they had were green peppers and turnips.

A large burlap sack had a handwritten label that said, "Brad and David's stinky fertilizer." A small sign listed the ingredients ("unadulterated crap") and said the men produced it themselves. Somehow, I doubted that.

Brad noticed me first. "Hey, Mel, how are you and Ambrose?"

David added, "Sure sorry you had to find old Mr. Frost."

"So were we. I wanted to ask…"

Brad interrupted me. "Do you know how he died?"

"No, and I wish the sheriff would figure it out." I spoke more abruptly than I intended, but I didn't want to talk more about Peter Frost.

David spoke before Brad could ask another question. "You in the market for some of our stuff?"

"Just a couple of bags. I have a good-sized garden behind Mrs. Keyser's house."

We talked price for a minute, and they came down a little when I offered them any tomatoes I hadn't sold by the end of the market. Since everyone sold them, I knew I would have at least a few left.

Sandi stopped by just before the market ended at three. By that time, the heat had begun to wilt any flowers or bedding vegetables that were not under a canopy. She wore a sundress and had her auburn hair in a French braid that made her look about eighteen. She laughed at one of Sam's jokes, and they chatted as I packed a basket to give to Brad and David.

I had too much to take back to my pickup in one basket, so I left Sandi and walked to within a few feet from David and Brad's table. They appeared to be wrapping up a deal with a scrawny woman who looked to be about forty.

The customer wanted them to deliver their product, and they were balking. When David saw me looking in their direction, he nodded and ended their conversation by saying they would drop off what she needed tonight.

I couldn't blame the woman for wanting it delivered. I didn't look forward to putting the stuff in my truck, even though it wasn't supposed to smell much once it had been aged enough to sell.

Brad pointed out their panel truck, and I drove my pickup to park beside it. After a couple minutes of me moving gardening equipment around, Brad threw two large burlap sacks of truly foul crap into the pickup.

I pinched my nose, mostly to make a point, since I could move a few feet to avoid the smell. "How long have you guys let this stuff sit?"

Brad grinned. "Not quite a year. That's why it's such a good deal."

I didn't say anything else. If I'd known it smelled as if it just came from the cow, I would have bought the stuff elsewhere. I'd have to make sure I emptied the pickup tonight. By tomorrow, even the cab would stink.

Sam had packed up when I got back to the table, so Sandi helped me carry two empty bushel baskets and a sack of peppers and onions back to my truck. I thought maybe she had learned something new, but she was just bored on a lazy Sunday afternoon.

"Will you let me read Hal's book when you get it Monday?"

"You're a glutton for punishment."

She shrugged. "If it's not related to Frost's death, it could be good for a laugh."

I decided not to say that nothing struck me funny right now.

CHAPTER SIX

SHERIFF GALLAGHER FROWNED when he saw me Monday morning. Or maybe his irritation stemmed from not being able to "put his hands" on Hal's manuscript. It ticked me off that he tried to make me feel guilty about it.

"I wished you'd told me right away, Melanie. Would have helped." He stood from behind his desk. "Wait a sec while I see if Sophie has it."

He left the office door open, so I didn't try to look at the files stacked neatly on his desk. I glanced at the plaque on the wall behind it, which proclaimed him a member in good standing in the Iowa Sheriff's Association.

Gallagher ambled back a minute later, manila folder in hand. "Found it in the evidence locker." He glanced at a tag on the front before he tore it off. "Good place for it, since the truck stayed in the lot overnight. Sorry for the delay."

I stood and took it. "No problem." Our eyes met. "Any news on who killed Mr. Frost?"

He held my gaze for just a second and looked back at this desk. "I think we're getting closer. Won't know much for a day or so."

I didn't ask for details, since I knew he wouldn't answer. "How's Granger holding up?"

Gallagher shook his head as he sat back down. "Tough. May get easier after the funeral tomorrow."

I hadn't given Frost's funeral a thought. Why would I? "It does. But it takes a while."

I decided not to add that I didn't give a damn about anything for six months after my parents' funerals.

STOOPER WAS WORKING AT Syl's place, and I planned for Mister Tibbs and me to join him after we visited some businesses on the square.

Seeing a newsstand with Monday's *South County News* deterred me for a bit. I put fifty cents in the metal coin slot and pulled out a paper.

A two-inch headline blared, "**Local Farmer Found Dead in Neighbor's Barn.**" I scanned the article. It mentioned that Aaron Granger, Ambrose and I had arrived at essentially the same time, and that Ambrose had removed the knife.

However, most of the article was a statement from Sheriff Gallagher saying in fifty words or so that he didn't know much. Nothing implied that Ambrose had anything to do with Frost's murder.

I breathed more easily and bent down to pet the leashed Mister Tibbs. "Maybe it'll be okay."

She cocked her head at me, and I turned toward the local dollar store. A bike rack sits a few yards from the entrance. Mister Tibbs would be okay there for two or three minutes.

Jagdish Patel owns shops in several small towns in South County as well as nearby Van Buren and Lee Counties. He told me once that none made enough to justify staying in business, but together they let him stay solvent. Plus, it kept two brothers-in-law employed.

I'd sat in a couple of council meetings in a few towns when they discussed leasing him a building that had come back to a town because of a tax lien. Some people grumbled about the low rent they charged him, but the alternative meant another vacant building. We have plenty of those already.

I appreciated the cool air that greeted me as I entered the small store. With its wood floors and ceiling fans, Patel's shop is more like the variety stores of old than the chain dollar stores of today.

On one side are modern beauty products, on the other side household and cleaning products. In the middle are packaged foods that lean toward sugar and salt, plus toys and craft supplies.

Patel's sing-song Indian accent greeted me. "Good morning, Miss Reporter."

I did a small wave. "Gardener, remember?"

"Oh, sure. Can I help you?"

"I need toothpaste, and then I have a proposition for you."

His smile became more perfunctory. There aren't many businesses in River's Edge compared to even fifteen years ago. People drive the few miles to larger towns so they have more selection and, usually, cheaper prices.

That means every sports team asks for donations for their jerseys. The Lions and Rotary Clubs or churches want discounts on paper goods for pancake breakfasts or bazaars.

I plopped the toothpaste on the wood counter. With its chipped, dark green paint, the counter is quite a contrast to the sleek cash register.

Mr. Patel walked over and picked up the toothpaste to scan it. "What's up?"

I explained my idea for the planters and quoted a price. "So, I'd bring them full of dirt and plant and water them. You'd keep watering them, so no monthly service fee or anything like that."

"That'll be two-ten." He bagged the toothpaste, clearly pondering. "That's not bad. I'll do it. You plant them again next year?"

"Sure. I'll give you a price before I do it."

He took my money and handed me the bag. "What I really need is someone to scrape the paint around the big window, then caulk and repaint."

I didn't relish that kind of work. "What about Stooper? He's been helping me a lot at Syl Seaton's place."

Patel's expression could be described as pained, so I continued. "He drinks less. Always on time. You can check with Syl if you like."

"He's new, so I'd take your word first. Have Stooper stop by."

BY THE TIME I swung into Syl's driveway, I'd also secured planter placements from the drug store and Chamber of Commerce.

The craft store and the tiny coffee shop had turned me down, but I bet they'd have their own flowers in front before I could provide mine. Mine would look better.

Mister Tibbs stood in the back seat, tail wagging and paws on the window, which was not much bigger than her head.

"Okay, girl, you can chase squirrels, but stay where I can see you." I opened my door, and she hopped onto the front seat and out the door in two seconds.

"So much for being attached to me," I muttered.

Stooper had left Syl's before I arrived, or perhaps he had put the trellises in Sunday. On his own, obviously. They looked good, though the roses had not yet been threaded throughout the slats.

Syl's snazzy truck sat at the end of the driveway. He was obviously working at home rather than in Des Moines. As I parked, he walked out the front door and onto the wide porch.

"Morning, Melanie." He nodded at the trellises. "Good to see the progress."

I walked backwards toward the porch, inspecting whether the trellises were evenly spaced on each side of the front gate. They were.

"Thanks to Stooper. I bought them, but he did the hard work." I turned to face Syl.

He had what could be described as an ear-to-ear grin. "Heard you stepped in it again."

I shook my head. "You better watch it. You're sounding like a farmer."

"Hey, you're a farmer."

I frowned. "I hope to be again. I can't tell you how appalled Ambrose and I felt to find Peter Frost in the barn like that."

He grew somber. "I'm sure. What would have brought him to your barn?"

"No one knows. Kind of odd, but maybe he saw something he thought needed checking." I used this line to anyone who asked. It encompassed any possibility, and was the kind of neighborly thing most farmers would do. Except Peter Frost had not been that kind of neighbor.

Syl gestured to a porch chair, and we both sat. "How's your brother? I read in the paper that he found the man."

"Other than irritated that the sheriff has implied Ambrose might actually have killed Frost, he's okay."

"Humph. Hard to imagine."

"I'm trying to look at it from the law's perspective. Next week we had a scheduled hearing about whether Frost had a leg to stand on for his claims on the property. People who don't know us could say we had a reason to want the guy dead."

"Gone on for a while, hasn't it?"

"Seems like forever, but it's only been a couple of years." I looked at the neat gardens in Syl's front yard and thought how barren the area around my parents' house looked. My mother always had flowers blooming, but Ambrose and I just paid people to mow.

"Our lawyer thinks a judge will throw out the claim. Would have happened earlier, but Frost's lawyer got a couple postponements."

"Did he think you and Ambrose would give in if it went on?"

I nodded. "We thought so. It bothered both of us, probably Ambrose more. He worked those fields with my Dad a lot more than I did."

Syl looked at me and turned away as he asked, "So what happens now?"

"I haven't had time to talk to Ken Brownberg, but I can't imagine Frost's estate pursuing it."

I assumed Frost left everything to Granger, who had never farmed. He probably knew most local farmers thought Frost's claim was a bald-faced lie.

With land prices going up and down with the price of corn, it would be a heck of a headache for Granger to fight for something that might not earn him a profit. Ambrose and I would run the farm ourselves, so we wouldn't be paying for the kind of labor Granger would have to.

I realized I'd been silent for as much as a minute and looked at Syl. I'd expected his sometimes irreverent smirk, but his eyes implied sympathy.

He looked away. "I hope you get it resolved quickly."

I stood. "I bought some good organic fertilizer at the farmers' market yesterday. Used most at my place, but I saved a little for those tomatoes behind your house."

"Sure. Put it on your next bill."

"God no." I grinned. "Plus, I'd have to charge you for the stink."

He frowned as he stood. "Great. I'll go close the kitchen windows."

I drove my truck closer to the back of Syl's house and took the wheelbarrow from the small barn behind the house. Since Stooper and I worked so much at Syl's, I kept a few things on hand. Mostly items that were a pain to haul in and out of my pickup.

By the time I finished spreading the stuff, the bright sun beat down. Stooper would be here soon, and we could work together to get some of the roses off the white wood fence. Though the blooms were strewn along the fence, the bases of the plants were near the trellises.

My phone rang as I pushed the wheelbarrow toward the barn.

"Melanie? Sheriff Gallagher here."

"Hi. You find the killer?"

"We think so. I'm calling as a courtesy. I asked the police in Dubuque to arrest Ambrose."

CHAPTER SEVEN

I SAT ON THE ground next to the wheel barrow, feeling light-headed and completely helpless.

Gallagher had said if "everything went as planned" he'd let me talk to Ambrose in the county jail after six.

I called Ken Brownberg to get a recommendation for a criminal attorney. Because he had a name and phone number immediately, he must have thought Ambrose's arrest more likely than I had. Ken said the lawyer from Fairfield would talk to Ambrose before he was arraigned in River's Edge.

"Do you know the charge?" I asked.

After a few seconds of silence, he said, "I've heard second-degree murder."

Though I didn't like Brownberg's information, I thanked him and asked who he had recommended.

"Charlotte Dickey, and I would use her myself if I needed such representation."

I had to purse my lips not to tell him to sound less snarky. I had enough self-control to know the reaction was probably more my perception than his intended tone.

Next, I called my sister-in-law, but the call went to voice mail. I didn't know what Sharon would know yet, so I chose my words carefully. "I'm reminding you that I have an extra bedroom if you need it. I won't even make you share it with Mister Tibbs. Call me, okay?"

I wanted to ask her if she'd gotten a different lawyer for Ambrose, but she was probably still teaching and wouldn't have had time. She or Ambrose would probably call Ken and get the same recommendation.

I was still sitting on the ground when Syl opened the side door to his house. He walked quickly down the steps toward me, holding up his house phone. "Sandi. She said she couldn't get through on your cell."

I whispered. "Did she tell you?"

He nodded. "I'm sorry."

My eyes filled. "It's not true."

He stooped and put a hand on my shoulder, handing the phone to me as he did. "I'm sure you're right."

I gulped a sob. "Sandi? What do you know?"

A wet feeling at my elbow made me look down. Mister Tibbs' head was cocked, and if a dog can look concerned, she did. Syl reached over and scratched her head.

Sandi spoke fast. "Ryan's mother's cousin at the sheriff's office said that a lot had to do with Ambrose's fingerprints on the knife. How he was holding it."

I almost smiled at the idea that one of Gallagher's deputies was passing information to a reporter. "What does that mean?"

Syl stood and extended a hand. I took it and stood.

"I'm not sure," Sandi said.

"Give me a minute." I closed my eyes, envisioning the scene the day we found Peter Frost.

Frost was on the barn floor, lying between Ambrose and where Granger and I stood. Ambrose knelt next to Frost, with the knife in his right hand.

How was he holding the knife?

Ambrose's palm extended over the knife hilt, with his pinky near the blade. His thumb was wrapped around the hilt, coming to rest near the edge of his curled fingers. A murderer might have used the same method to grasp and thrust a knife, but how else might Ambrose have held it to remove the knife?

With a sick feeling, I realized I would have grasped it almost the opposite, with my thumb and index finger close to the blade. Sort of a backhand grip. That didn't mean everyone would have handled the knife my way to remove it.

Or to stab someone. In fact, on TV I thought murderers held a knife quite differently and thrust in and up. But those attacks were generally planned.

Ambrose didn't plot to stab Frost in a certain way. He wasn't a killer.

I felt chilled. Ambrose was right-handed. If he had removed the knife with his left hand, the sheriff and his deputies might have figured Ambrose would have had a hard time stabbing with that hand. But anyone would have used their dominant hand to remove the knife. There had to be more to it than that.

I opened my eyes. "Okay, Sandi, you might say he held it in a way that somebody could use it to kill Frost, but I thought that would also have been the most logical way to pull it out."

She blew out a breath. "Damn it, I wish he'd left it alone."

"Me, too. I'm going to see if Dr. MacGregor will let me read his ME report." I knew he wouldn't. I'd have to get it from Ambrose's lawyer. Assuming she would let me see it.

"Okay. I'll use any source I can, but the sheriff and his deputies have been really close-mouthed on this one."

I pushed the end button and turned to Syl, who stood a few feet away, staring at me as Mister Tibbs wound around his legs.

I handed Syl his phone. "Thanks."

He frowned. "Drive me out to your parents' place. It's nearby, right?"

I hesitated. "The police tape might still be up."

"Or might not. You'll feel better if you're doing something."

I started to say I wanted to be anywhere but that barn, but maybe Syl and I would see something the sheriff missed. Not likely, but worth a try.

"Okay. Let's take your truck."

When Syl gave me a sort of questioning look, I added, "No one will think much if you drive onto the property. Probably lots of people are, if the place isn't cordoned off. My pickup might get noticed more."

He went to get his keys, and I looked down at Mister Tibbs. "You have to stay on my lap. And don't try to lick Syl when he's driving."

I got her blanket and leash from my pickup and opened Syl's unlocked passenger door. I rarely do something a friend might resent, but I didn't want Syl to say that Mister Tibbs had to stay at his place.

Syl pulled the driver's door shut, looked at me cradling Mister Tibbs on his truck's front seat, and then turned to lock the door. I couldn't see his expression.

As Syl drove the couple miles to the farm, I stared at flat fields of corn and soybeans, not really seeing them. It made no sense. Even if Ambrose and I arrived close to the time someone killed Frost, we got the calls to go to the farm. We weren't lying in wait for Frost. Especially Ambrose. His drive from Dubuque had taken hours.

"Any ideas?" Syl asked.

"Surely they've looked at his phone to see what cell towers he used. They'll know he was on the road."

Syl turned into the farm. "They must think there is a very narrow window for time of death."

I thought about this as I got out of his truck. Reporters in small Iowa towns don't cover murders on anything like a regular basis. I remembered what Sandi had said about Frost's body temperature and suppressed a shiver.

I placed a leashed Mister Tibbs on the ground as my eyes swept the area between the house and barn. The main barn doors were closed. A short piece of yellow police tape hung loosely on the metal ring used to grip the barn door that faced the house and slide it along its metal track. The tape dangled as if left behind.

I walked to the barn, Syl a pace or two behind me and Mister Tibbs straining on her leash ahead of me. She had wanted to go in this barn for a long time, but I never let her.

I yanked on the ring, and the door slid on its track as I pulled it open.

Syl had been taking in the house, barn, and cornfield that came almost up to the back of the barn. He looked into the barn itself. "Dark place."

"I'll open the back door, so there'll be light from two sides." I looked down at Mister Tibbs. "Can you hold her leash for a second?"

He took it, and I shook a finger at her. "Stay down."

I walked the sixty feet across the barn, glancing right and left. Even in the dim light, a chalk outline showed how Frost's body had lain. I forced my eyes from it and slid the back door along its track. Light beamed in, but not as brightly as with the front door, since the tall corn stalks were close to the back of the barn.

I met Syl and Mister Tibbs at the center of the building, where Syl looked up.

I could have told him that many years ago a second level was beneath the steep roof. It covered maybe a quarter of the space, and wasn't closed in.

Mostly the second tier was used to store bales of hay, since it was drier than on the ground. When the wood started to rot, my father tore it down and didn't replace it. He could make more in corn and soybeans, so he got rid of the animals.

"Does it look the same?" Syl asked.

"I hadn't been in here for two years until the day somebody murdered Frost." I described why I thought boxes might have been stored on the floor. "Now, you can't really tell because there are hundreds of footprints from the sheriff's people and EMTs."

"And last you knew it was empty?"

"Yes. But with the corn this high, if someone pulled around to the back, they wouldn't be visible from the road. Keep the front door shut, and you'd be in your own little world."

"Well, if nothing should be here, I'll walk one side and you walk the other."

His matter-of-fact approach had a calming effect. "Sounds good. Come on Mister Tibbs."

I walked back to the front door, and then she and I walked slowly on our side. I looked at the floor, and Mister Tibbs sneezed several times as she smelled every inch of the dirt.

Near the far end of the barn, she stopped walking and smelled vigorously. I figured she'd found a mouse scent and bent over to gently raise her head.

A dark spot on the dirt caught my eye. The black spot was about the size of a half-dollar, not even an inch from the wall.

At my height, I'd missed it. I stooped next to Mister Tibbs and ran my hand down her back. "Good girl."

I squatted and wriggled the dirt until I had some on my finger. It looked like the black powder used in ammunition, though it didn't have the acrid smell of a fired gun. Another faint odor seemed familiar, but I couldn't quite place it.

It's not uncommon to have explosives on a farm, especially if water runs through the property and beavers build dams. However, my father had only kept a couple of rifles to kill coyotes that went after dogs or chickens.

I sniffed again. The black residue smelled like sulfur, but not as much as the stink bombs always produced at the high school on April Fool's Day.

The black powder could have had a lot of uses, but my Dad would never have kept any of it in the barn.

Temperatures fluctuated too much, and super high temps could contribute to a fire.

Syl spoke from behind me. "Find something?"

Lost in my thoughts, I almost fell over with surprise. "Mister Tibbs did." I stood and held out my hand. "Some black powder. Probably nothing, but I don't know why...wait a minute."

The sound of a couple of roman candles whizzing around the farm yard came to me. "Somebody shot off a couple of roman candles out here the other day. I bet they were using the barn."

"Shooting them in here? This wood would go up pretty fast if it ran into sparks."

I wiped my hands on my jeans. "I bet someone hid stuff in here while they got ready to sell it. Kids drive down to Missouri and come back with a trunk full of stuff to light around Fourth of July."

Syl glanced around the barn. "I guess Missouri's not that far. I didn't look for anything as fine as black powder. I'll walk my part again."

I stood silently, thinking and gazing around the barn. Whatever brought people here, there couldn't have been a lot of traffic. Neighbors would have noticed.

Vacant properties attracted bored teenagers and the occasional hitchhiker or homeless person. Most weren't destructive, but some were. But the barn had no damage, not even trash lying around.

Somebody cleaned up.

That reinforced that whoever had been in here, whether the day of the murder or prior to it, used the barn for something illegal. If it had been a meth lab, the smell might have carried to other farms. At least to the road. Plus, methamphetamine makers were notoriously careless and messy.

"Oh." I stooped and picked up Mister Tibbs. The chemicals used to make meth were really dangerous, not for a dog's nose. Perhaps the barn had not been a meth kitchen.

Mister Tibbs did not want to be held. After a few seconds, I reasoned that if chemical residue was on the floor, it would deter her from sniffing a spot. I put her down.

I walked to the barn's back door, and Syl called from the front. "Don't see anything except a bunch of footprints from all the police and ambulance guys."

"Same here." I stared at the cornfield, which started about six feet behind the barn. The corn rose above my head. Movies show people running through the stalks, but they don't depict the real world, where thick groups of plants are unyielding and can easily cut any uncovered skin.

I didn't think anyone had used the field for cover. No, if they came into the barn they would probably drive a car or truck behind it and go in through the back door. With the front door shut, no one would see them.

Syl joined me and stared into the fields. "Meditating?"

"Ruminating. Someone used this barn. Maybe not the day Frost was killed, but they were doing something."

Syl walked to my right, and something he did made a clicking sound. "Why didn't you say there was a light?"

I looked at the wall he stood near. Two small, round lights, evidently battery operated, hung on the wall at a height of about seven feet. They were the kind that you turned on and off by pushing on the small, plastic globe.

"Because we only had one electric light in here, and the electricity's been off for ages."

Syl pulled one light off the wall. It had been affixed with Velcro and made a sort of sandpaper-on-wood sound as he removed it. "Bet there were more."

"Agreed." I scanned the barn. "Wish I had the high-beam flashlight I keep in the truck."

Syl had a wimpy flashlight in his glove box, but it shone more brightly than a mobile phone's screen. Twenty minutes later the barn was full of dog prints, and we had found several more spots that had Velcro on the wall, the lights having been removed.

"You know," I said, "they must have used these only during daylight. If there had been lights on in the barn at night, someone would've called me."

"Maybe," Syl said, "but these weren't powerful lights. I doubt anyone would notice if only one was lit. Now what?"

I took my phone from the back pocket of my jeans. "I'm playing by the rules. Maybe the sheriff can find some fingerprints near where the lights were."

CHAPTER EIGHT

TO SAY THE SHERIFF was furious when I finished telling him what we had found would be a world class understatement. Gallagher was red-faced and yelling loud enough to be heard at the diner.

I stared at him. My face burned red, but I didn't want to rage back. I wanted him to check the lights. "I don't get why you're mad at us. You took down the yellow tape."

Gallagher turned to Syl. "I don't know you well Mr. Seaton, but I would've thought you had more sense than to visit a crime scene."

Syl's expression was impassive. "I didn't buy a ticket on your railroad."

It took me a couple of seconds to get it, and I laughed.

It took Gallagher a few more, and he didn't.

"I'm not railroading anyone, goddammit! Evidence is evidence."

"You missed some," Syl said.

Gallagher took a breath and struggled to lower his voice. "We may have. If so, we'll revisit."

I crossed my arms across my chest. "I think that black powder means someone had, I don't know, guns or fireworks or something in that barn."

He jabbed an intercom button on his phone. "Get me Harmon, will you Sophie?" He looked back at me. "There's probably a small amount of black powder on every barn floor in the county."

"Except for the Amish," Syl said.

I suppressed a grin.

Gallagher glared at him. "I saw those bulbs. Figured they'd been there."

I wanted to learn what Gallagher knew, so I kept my tone even. "I get that, but the fact that they came on after being in a vacant barn for a couple of years tells us they had fresh batteries."

He ran a hand over his beefy face and walked to the chair behind his desk. "Sit down. I want to know what you disturbed in the barn."

I flushed, and sat. Syl leaned against the wall. "I'll stand."

I decided not to mention Mister Tibbs. "We didn't…" I began.

Newt Harmon walked in, and Gallagher pointed a finger at him. "Get out to the Perkins' barn with some fingerprint dust and see what you can pick up at…" he pulled a piece of paper from a drawer and thrust it and a pencil toward me, "near some Velcro on the wall."

To me, he added, "Draw a diagram and put x's about where you saw the sticky stuff."

Harmon looked puzzled, but stood silently while I drew a rectangle with open spaces for the two doors, and marked the Velcro spots.

I turned and handed it to the deputy. "In the back you'll see two small lights near the door. They're round, battery operated. My family didn't install those. Syl and I touched the one on the right."

A harsh voice came from the doorway. "What were you doing in that barn?"

I turned to see Aaron Granger's frown and rigid posture.

"I wanted to see if I could spot something to clear Ambrose."

"Granger," Gallagher began, "you need to let me handle this."

He reddened. "You're letting her prowl…"

Gallagher cut him off. "If you think I don't know how to run an investigation, you have another thought coming. Back off."

Granger turned and left, fury radiating from his departing back.

Newt Harmon nodded at Gallagher and, with my diagram protruding from the pocket of his tan uniform shirt, followed Granger.

The palpable three-second pause in the room felt like time sitting in the corner as a childhood punishment.

Finally, Gallagher said, "I believe the facts support your brother's arrest. I will examine new evidence."

He pointed a finger at me, continuing my feeling of being scolded.

"But I have to be the one to find it. Right now, if something about those lights would exonerate Ambrose, it might be thrown out because you found them."

I sat up straighter. "But..."

"No buts," Gallagher said.

He looked at Syl. "I can't tell you where to go or not go, Mr. Seaton, but I advise you, both of you, to leave this to the police and the lawyers."

I TRIED TO QUELL SOME of my anger by working with Stooper for two hours as he finished planting at Dr. Carver's. I glanced at my watch. Almost three-thirty.

When all the plants were in and some mulch spread, Stooper and I took the fifty yards or so of edging and began to insert it at the edge of the gardens. I had tried to tell Dr. Carver to save her money. Most weeds spread their seeds via air rather than roots.

She had not been persuaded. I certainly didn't mind the work.

I stood to stretch just as my phone rang. Sharon's voice asked, "Melanie? You've heard then?"

"Yes, but I didn't know if you had, so I left the message about my extra room."

"I'm driving down now. Depending on what happens at tonight's arraignment, I may take you up on it. Ken Brownberg said he got a lawyer who will meet us when Ambrose is booked in."

"I'm sorry, Sharon."

"It'll be okay."

I felt a lump rising in my throat. "How can you be so sure?"

"I refuse to believe my husband will be convicted of a murder he didn't commit."

I didn't share her sentiment, but refrained from saying so. "So, meet you in the courthouse?"

A horn honked on Sharon's end. "I shouldn't talk and drive. See you at six."

I looked around for Stooper. When I arrived I had given him the run down about Ambrose's arrest, but all he'd done was mutter about rushing to judgment.

Stooper stood by his beat-up car getting a drink from a water jug. Not that I would mind him overhearing a conversation with Sharon. He's become my friend. A friend I would not have expected to have.

I knelt again and tried to focus on loosening the soil with a trowel to lay the edging evenly. I didn't give a damn about Dr. Carver's edging, but it paid the bills.

Stooper and I worked without talking for another ten minutes, so his voice startled me as much as his question.

"So, if Ambrose didn't do it, who did?"

I wiped my brow with the small towel I have on a belt loop when I'm working. "I don't know. I think someone used the barn. Needless to say, without our permission."

"For what?"

"Not sure. I found a little bit of black powder near one wall. I wonder if someone was making or storing fireworks."

"'Round here anybody dumb enough to make 'em would've probably blowed themselves up."

I laughed, but stopped, thinking. "I saw Nelson and his cousin, Harlan I think his name is, at the hardware store a couple of days ago. Nelson's usually got some scheme going on, doesn't he?"

Stooper almost snorted. "He wouldn't have the brains to make 'em. His cousin I don't know. Not from around here, is he?"

"Missouri."

Stooper stopped pressing edging into the dirt. "Guess the cousin could be bringing them up."

"Iowa cops watch some of the roads to make sure fireworks aren't smuggled in." I frowned. "Kind of hard to do it."

"Somebody's really organized about it, they wouldn't buy boxes of the stuff at that big red place just into Missouri."

I envisioned the bright red building, easily three times the size of our barn. "Good point." I stood and brushed off my knees. "I think I'll hang out at the hardware store for a few minutes."

Stooper grinned. "Andy'll love it."

I went over the "barn as fireworks hideout" idea as I drove toward the hardware store. Just about every main road into Missouri from Iowa has a huge fireworks sales point within a half-mile of the border. They were all open now.

You can buy sparklers in Iowa and charcoal snakes, but other fireworks are outlawed, except big displays by licensed vendors. I don't think much about them except to go to the annual displays in River's Edge.

I certainly didn't give illegal fireworks transport much thought. I've heard that for a few months every year, bringing in fireworks from Missouri can be as big a smuggling operation as bargain cigarettes.

I decided that before going to the hardware store I'd see what I could learn from Sandi. I'd expected to hear more from her or Ryan by now and wondered what they were up to.

The bell above the glass door tinkled as I walked into the *South County News* office. My eyes strayed across the area with reporters' desks, the so-called bullpen. Betty, the lifestyle columnist, sat at her desk near the back of the large room.

She's in her fifties and never acts happy about working, even though she gets to go to local school and social events. Betty had headphones on and was intent on her computer screen.

I could have made off with the laptop sitting on a desk near the door.

Scott Holmes walked out of the editor's office, and I held up a hand in greeting. He nodded and walked toward me. He carries himself with almost regal bearing, but I wouldn't say he acts stuffy. He's just a lot more formal than most people in town.

"Hello, Melanie. May I help you?"

He had almost reached me, and I realized his tight smile didn't reach his eyes.

"I wanted to talk to Sandi or Ryan. Or you," I added as an afterthought. "I can't figure out why Sheriff Gallagher arrested my brother."

His expression relaxed somewhat, and for a second, I thought I saw sympathy in his eyes. "I'm sure you'll catch up with them, but our work and your investigation have to be separate."

It took me a couple of seconds to get that he'd told Ryan and Sandi not to talk to me about what they found out. "Oh." Then I started to get mad. "Does that mean you don't want to know if I find out anything?"

He drew a breath that was almost a sigh. "No. It does mean that you turned down Doc Shelton's offer to serve as acting editor and that Sandi and Ryan are the reporting team on this."

I blinked and stood very still.

When I said nothing, he added, "I hope your brother is cleared of this. From what I've heard people say about him in the last couple of hours, he seems an unlikely murderer."

Had Holmes said anything besides hoping Ambrose was innocent, I might have told him to get off his high horse. Or maybe get on it and ride out of town. Instead, I said, "It does make sense. Okay."

He half-smiled. "I'm certainly not telling your friends to avoid you at Mason's Diner."

I thanked him and left. I felt more alone than at any time in the two years since my parents died.

CHAPTER NINE

THE FRONT OF THE hardware store sported red, white, and blue bunting. Given the upcoming holiday, a small trash can held flags on thin wooden poles. A few sad-looking tomato plants and geraniums sat next to the flags and lawn mowers.

The air conditioning felt good when I walked in, a welcome relief from the hot, muggy air.

Andy had the *South County News* spread on the cash register counter. He started to close it, then recognized me. "Paper didn't say Ambrose did it."

Implied in his statement was that Andy thought it possible. I stopped walking and stared at him.

Andy shrugged. "Course, you wouldn't think he did."

"I know so, emphasis on know."

"Did you bail him out yet?"

God give me strength. "He isn't in town yet."

Then it hit me. Bail money. I had focused on getting him a lawyer, not getting him out of jail. Did Sharon have enough money on hand?

Something about my posture or frown seemed to quell Andy's questions about Ambrose, because he said, "Need something, Mel?"

"Just bought some fertilizer from Brad and David, but I didn't get quite enough. You carry anything organic?" I knew they didn't, so I wouldn't have to walk out with any smelly stuff.

"Nope." He jerked behind him, with his thumb. "But we got some regular fertilizer back there."

Andy's customer service skills were good only if he wanted to chat. Since he knew I didn't, he was again immersed in the paper before I'd gone a few steps.

I walked around the gardening area inspecting pots I could use for my streetscape project. I needed an excuse to ask Andy if he knew much about Nelson's activities these days. No way could I ask if he thought Nelson had been using our barn to store fireworks.

I picked up an eight-inch pot made of heavy plastic and carried it to the counter. Andy didn't even look up until I set it on his newspaper.

"You know if the store can order these in a larger size, maybe twenty-four inches in diameter, a couple of feet tall?"

He looked dubious. "Be a darn big pot. Whatcha want it for?"

"Just for some of the places I'm working. Can you do it?"

"I hafta ask the boss. He does the orderin'." He picked up the small pot. "You want this?"

"Nope. It's for you to use to ask about larger ones."

He placed it behind him, in a cart used to move stock around the store. I didn't have high hopes for him remembering to ask about a different size.

"So, Andy, I hadn't seen Nelson in a long time. He come in a lot?"

Andy's eyebrows went up. "How come you want to know?"

"Might need some more help if I get another big project."

Andy frowned. "Not sure you want to use him. Kinda light-fingered, you know?"

I smiled. "I heard. Haven't seen his name in the paper for a while."

"He's got some kind of thing going. Him and Harlan need to load a truck."

That caught my interest. "With what?"

He shook his head. "Didn't care to ask."

"In other words, you weren't supposed to be listening."

Andy straightened his shoulders. "You saying I eavesdropped? That's..." He seemed to search for a word.

"Offensive? Insulting?" I said this with a smile, and he relaxed.

"I like to know what's goin' on. See, you do, too, or you wouldn't ask."

I turned toward the door, saying, "If you think Nelson's still practicing his old trade, you don't need to tell him I asked about him."

I SHOWERED AND CHANGED into blue twill slacks and a sleeveless peach top, complemented by a tan linen jacket. I generally don't think much about how I look, but I took time drying my hair and put on mascara.

Though she had enjoyed having me around, Mister Tibbs was not happy that I walked her around the block and then wanted to put her back in the apartment. "I'll make it up to you later, girl."

She whined, something she hasn't done since the first day I found her in Syl's barn. She sat on her blanket and looked up with the kind of baleful eyes only a dog has.

I sat on the floor next to her. I wear dark pants because I can usually count on Mister Tibbs sharing dog hair.

"I'll tell you what, girl. You can sleep in my room tonight. Come on." I stood and snapped my fingers.

When she wagged her tail, I picked up her blanket. I needed to get her out of the living room in case Sharon spent the night. Might as well act as if she was getting a treat.

She trotted ahead of me and started to go in the guest bedroom. "Nope. Come on, Mister Tibbs." I put her blanket on my mother's old hope chest and sat a ladder-back chair next to it. She could get on the chair and then the chest to look out the window.

In two bounces she clambered to her blanket, very proud of herself. Her short tail wagged so fast it almost blurred.

"Okay, you can stay there 'til I come back."

This did not please her, but a bird flew by the window and distracted her.

I went quickly down the exterior stairs and pulled out of the driveway before Mrs. Keyser could come onto her porch.

Though the building I headed toward is called the courthouse, it's actually the two-story county office building, which happens to house two courtrooms. It's next to what is formally called the law enforcement building, which houses the sheriff's office and an eight-bed jail.

As I got closer to the courthouse, I noted the heavier-than-usual traffic, so I slowed.

Within several seconds, I realized two television vans and a batch of people stood near the entrance. I could tell they were reporters by the mix of khaki pants and bored postures.

"Damn." I turned right on the street before the courthouse and drove a block before parking. I would probably know reporters from Keosauqua or Fairfield. Certainly the TV reporter from Quincy, Candi Spright, would recognize me. I hadn't seen her stylish clothes in the group or her casually attired cameraman, Bob, who usually sported deck shoes and faded jeans.

With my dressier cloths and nicely styled hair, I hoped out-of-town reporters wouldn't recognize me easily. If they had thought to ask anyone what I looked like, they would have been told I wore cut-offs or jeans and tee shirts.

I didn't feel important. I simply knew reporters would expect me to talk to them since I used to be in the same business.

As I got closer to the courthouse, I didn't see Sandi.
Ryan's car was parked near the building. Sharon must have
driven it down, which meant the sheriff had released
Ambrose's car. Or they were spending the night with me
and I would drive them back to Dubuque tomorrow.

My eyes again roamed the area for Sandi, but no luck.
Despite Holmes' edict, I thought she'd tell me if she found
out something important about Ambrose. Or maybe I was
kidding myself.

Ambrose. I couldn't imagine his thoughts or emotions.
When I tried, the predominant feeling was despair. I
winced. I couldn't add to my own frustration and anger by
imagining my brother's.

I wished I'd thought to arrive a lot earlier. I punched
Sharon's phone number.

"Melanie?" she asked. "Good. I'm already in."

"It looks like the reporters are mostly near the side
door by the sheriff's place. I guess they expect Gallagher to
walk Ambrose over."

"They do, but Gallagher brought him over about forty
minutes ago."

"Have you seen him?"

"Not to talk. He's with that lawyer Ken recommended."

"Good. I'll come in the main door and meet you by the
courtroom."

The flight of steps into the courthouse is short, and I
reached the top before I heard Candi's voice call, "Melanie.
Oh Melanie!"

I ignored her and went inside.

After a couple of blinks, I spotted Sharon outside the
larger of the two courtrooms, sitting on a wooden pew. The
pews came from a long-ago demolished church. I've always
thought they were perfect for the courthouse, where
anybody waiting to appear before a judge probably did
some praying.

Sharon had on a tailored gray suit and low heels, much dressier than her usual teaching attire. With her abnormally pale face framed by her dark hair, she looked grim, or as if she had the flu.

She stood and walked to me. We hugged for maybe five seconds, which is a while if you aren't usually huggers.

She pulled back and looked at me. "You okay?"

"I should ask you that."

We walked back to the pew. "I'm mad as six hornets that just had their nest knocked down."

I grinned as I sat next to her. "That's the spirit."

As I said this, I glanced down the hall and saw Newt Harmon leaning against a wall near the exit. My guess was he was there to be sure Ambrose didn't leave.

"Beats tears," Sharon said. "I cried almost the entire drive down here."

I gave her a one-armed hug. "Hey, did you drive Ryan's car?"

She nodded. "Sheriff said he had released Ambrose's and was having it put in your driveway. It's there, right?"

"It wasn't there a few minutes ago, but if Gallagher says it'll be there, it will."

I figured he would have the car driven to my place so there wouldn't be attention from reporters later, when Sharon or I moved it from his lot. Any other time I would have thanked him. Today, I wanted to slug him for arresting Ambrose.

Sharon and I sat silently for maybe half a minute. I looked at Sharon's profile without turning my head. I'd never seen her look so haggard.

"Listen, Sharon, I hear everyone in town thinks it's ridiculous."

She nodded. "Supposedly the county attorney has to tell the judge a couple of reasons why they arrested Ambrose and make a bail recommendation."

Uh oh. County Attorney Smith and I had butted heads previously. I didn't believe he would hold that against Ambrose, but I thought Smith could be pig-headed.

The door to the courtroom opened, and Sheriff Gallagher walked out. He nodded at Sharon and me and rapped on the door across the hall, which I knew to be a small conference room. Someone must have told him to come in, because he opened the door and walked part way into the room before stepping back into the hall.

He gestured to Sharon and me, and we walked toward him. As we reached him, Ambrose stepped into the hall. Gallagher said, "One minute."

I stood aside to let Sharon hug her husband. Her façade must have crumbled, because she gave a brief sob as Ambrose enveloped her. "It'll be okay." He looked across Sharon and winked at me.

Charlotte Dickey, I assumed that's who she was, came into the hall, nodded at me, and turned to the sheriff. "We're ready when the judge is."

Sharon sniffed loudly, and Ambrose said, "Come on, honey, buck up."

Sharon turned to precede Ambrose across the hall, staring stonily ahead as she passed Gallagher. "Buck up my ass."

Sharon and I stood to one side as Gallagher, Dickey, and Ambrose walked into the courtroom. We followed and sat in chairs behind the table at which Ambrose and his attorney sat.

The courtroom we were in was the more formal of the two, with a jury box on the far side and an elevated judge's bench. The dark wood, whether naturally so or darkened after decades of use, created a gloomy atmosphere.

County Attorney Smith and the only other attorney in his office sat at the second front table, quietly conferring. Sheriff Gallagher took a seat behind them.

I looked around. The only other people in the room were Gallagher's assistant, Sophie, and the court stenographer. Sophie had a tablet on her lap, apparently to take notes so the sheriff didn't have to.

I drew a breath of relief, but the feeling didn't last long. The back door, which led to the main hall, opened, and a slew of reporters walked in. Sandi and Ryan gave me what can only be called sympathetic looks, as they moved quickly to get one of the few seats in the room.

Two other print reporters, Buster from Keosauqua and Alberta from Fairfield, also made it to chairs, as did the Ottumwa television station crew.

Not so the Quincy crew, which is the over-the-air broadcast station we get best in River's Edge. I hid a smile. Candi probably wanted to make an entrance, not realizing the room's size. And, more important, no one cared.

A door that led to the judge's chamber opened, and his bailiff emerged. "All rise."

Judge Francis Morton, tall and red-headed, is the Iowa District Judge who serves South County and others nearby. He walked in quickly, robes billowing. No one in our family had appeared before him previously.

Ambrose rose with his attorney, and I stood, squeezing Sharon's hand. I remembered I hadn't asked her about bail money and felt panicked.

The bailiff indicated we should sit, and Judge Morton said this was not a hearing that would determine guilt, simply a presentation of information to determine if there would be "reason to hold Mr. Perkins, grant bail, or permit him to be freed on his own recognizance."

The judge's last statement initially made me feel better. Then I realized he likely used the same language even if the evidence was overwhelming, like someone had been caught on camera robbing a bank.

"Tell me what you have, Attorney Smith."

The county attorney began with basic information about how Mr. Frost had been found and that Ambrose held "the weapon that the medical examiner has determined was used to kill Mr. Frost."

Judge Morton looked around. "I would have expected the sheriff's deputy who encountered Mr. Perkins would be in this hearing."

Since the judge had to know Granger was Frost's nephew, I would have thought Sheriff Gallagher would be allowed to state this.

After a brief pause, Ms. Dickey said, "The defense is willing to stipulate that Mr. Frost's nephew, Deputy Granger, was the first member of law enforcement on the scene."

The judge looked mildly amused. "Not a trial Attorney Dickey, but thank you." He nodded at Smith to continue.

Smith noted Frost appeared to have died "within the last few minutes before Deputy Granger arrived on the scene." He described Ambrose's position next to the body, holding the knife, and said that "the accused claims to have been called to the barn by Mr. Frost."

I was no legal expert, but nothing sounded like a firm reason to accuse Ambrose. Of course Frost had called Ambrose. Of course we would have gone to the farm, and of course Ambrose would have tried to help Peter Frost.

Attorney Smith shuffled a few papers and drew out one that I could see, even from a few yards away, had a star in the margin, mid-page.

"While the murder weapon in the hands of the accused is damning..."

Sharon flinched.

"...perhaps more so are statements that Mr. Perkins made about Mr. Frost's claim to have a verbal contract to sell the Perkins farm to him. A verbal contract made before the death of Martha and Arnold Perkins two years ago."

Judge Morton rolled his pointed finger, as if to hurry Smith's presentation. "And those statements were?"

Smith quoted Patrick Brannon, whom I knew to be the class clown in Ambrose's senior year. Brannon had told Sheriff Gallagher that Ambrose had said "nothing bad enough could happen to Frost," given what Frost had put Ambrose and me through.

I groaned internally. I could see Patrick feeling self-important at being interviewed and not realizing that his statement would contribute so much to Ambrose's arrest. Patrick might have even framed it as something funny. But the county attorney didn't take it that way.

"That's it?" the judge asked.

"No sir," Smith replied. "Mr. Perkins is also quoted as saying, "I'd kill the bastard, but they'd catch me.""

That caused paper shuffling and a couple of murmurs from reporters. I glanced at Sharon. She briefly shut her eyes.

Ambrose's attorney then described events as they had actually happened, saying that Ambrose's drive from Dubuque to River's Edge would not have allowed time to murder Peter Frost. "Even if my client were so inclined. Which he was not," she finished.

Dickey added that there was no direct evidence that Ambrose killed Frost and law enforcement had not made any effort to determine whether others might have been angry enough to kill the man.

Smith discounted Dickey's point that someone else killed Frost and then lured Ambrose and me to the barn to incriminate us. "In fact, counselor, Mr. Frost had called Deputy Granger, saying he was upset and wanted his nephew to come to the Perkins' barn."

Sharon and I both sat up straighter. All Gallagher had told me was something like Frost left a message and Granger couldn't reach him when he called back.

Judge Morton told both attorneys to "save it for a potential trial."

County Attorney Smith said he thought it was in the public interest that Ambrose remain in the county jail "as the case proceeds." He then added, "If your honor wishes to consider bail, the people ask that it be set at $500,000."

Charlotte Dickey raised her voice. "Your honor! Mr. Perkins has strong ties to this community and Dubuque. He did not commit this crime. In fact, the most serious crime he's committed was speeding on Interstate 80 five years ago."

Judge Morton looked steadily at County Attorney Smith. "That is a substantial sum. Explain your rationale."

"Though Mr. Perkins grew up here, he resides far outside this jurisdiction. Given that he lives on a farm, even wearing an ankle bracelet that permitted him to work his land would not be sufficient. He works independently. And the death threat was very specific."

Dickey straightened her shoulders. "Your Honor, most of us have said things after a few drinks that we wouldn't say otherwise. My client had no intention of acting on his comment."

"I don't," the judge said, frowning.

No one said anything as Judge Morton jotted a few notes on a legal pad in front of him.

He looked from Smith to Dickey and back to Smith. "While I understand your request for such a large amount, Mr. Perkins' lack of criminal history, the fact that he was on the road from Dubuque for several hours, and his full cooperation upon arrest lead me to set bail at $50,000."

Smith straightened his shoulders, but said nothing.

Morton glanced at Sheriff Gallagher as he spoke. "Given Mr. Perkins' lack of protest when he was arrested and absence of prior criminal activity, I'm inclined to let him return to Dubuque."

"Your honor…" Smith began.

"I hear you, Attorney Smith," Morton said. "But where's he going to go? Canada? His family and property are in Iowa."

A couple of reporters sniggered.

"Ankle bracelets have to be monitored constantly, and I don't think the expense is warranted. Sheriff Gallagher, I'd like you to make arrangements with the sheriff in Dubuque County to have Mr. Perkins check in daily, in person."

The judge looked at Ambrose. "Mr. Perkins, other than a daily visit to the sheriff, you are to stay on your farm unless you need medical care or plan to attend Sunday services. You are to inform the county attorney of any such plans, unless you are transported by ambulance. And then you or your family must call from the local hospital as soon as feasible."

Ambrose nodded, and his attorney said, "Thank you, your honor."

I thought Ambrose looked as pale as Peter Frost had been when we found him.

Judge Morton rapped the gavel, and the bailiff repeated his "all rise" call. The judge walked out, saying nothing more.

I didn't realize Sharon had been holding herself so tightly until I felt her relax. She hugged me, and I patted her shoulder blade.

Ambrose turned to Sharon with a questioning look at the same time a short, balding man walked in front of the cluster of reporters and came toward us. He nodded at Sharon.

When Smith had moved out of earshot, the man spoke in a low voice. "Told you. Let's get those papers signed."

I realized the man had to be a bail bondsman. He didn't live in River's Edge, unless he had moved here recently. I would remember anyone in their mid-thirties who wore button-down shirts and bow ties.

As he gestured that Sharon should accompany him to the defense table, a woman's voice said, "Melanie. Have you got a minute?"

Candi Spright had bugged me several times after Hal Morris' death a few months ago. While I found her bright-eyed style annoying, she had a job to do, and the easier I made it the better she would portray Ambrose.

"My brother or his wife might prefer to do the talking, so I'll just..."

"Bob." Without turning her head she gestured that her long-suffering cameraman should focus on me. "Let's start over, Melanie."

I glanced around the room. Ryan was following Smith out the door, and Sandi stood a couple of feet behind where Ambrose and Sharon were shaking hands with Dickey. The Ottumwa camerawoman and TV reporter were setting up closer to Ambrose. I hoped he could duck them.

Sheriff Gallagher was talking to Mr. Bail Bondsman and pointing in the direction of his office. I supposed that's where bail arrangements would be finalized.

My eyes met Candi's. She had been watching me, and I flushed.

With Bob's camera on me, she asked, "Were you surprised at your brother's arrest, Melanie?"

"As I said, I think Ambrose and his wife Sharon are the ones to talk to more than I. Ambrose and I both had calls to meet poor Mr. Frost the day someone murdered him, and we got there at almost the same time. Mr. Frost had already died."

"Sheriff's deputies maintain they found Ambrose Perkins holding the murder weapon."

"Removing the knife was a reflex action. Ambrose tried to help him."

"Yes, but..." Candi began.

Out of the corner of my eye, I saw Ambrose and Sharon walk out with Sheriff Gallagher and the bondsman.

"Really, Ms. Spright. My brother has been talking for himself all his life. He's the one you should interview."

She frowned and pushed the mic an inch or so closer to me. "But what about that threat?"

"It was more of an expression. Same as, 'I'd like to punch that reporter if she doesn't stop bugging me.'"

Bob sniggered, but the news producer could probably edit it out.

CHAPTER TEN

ALL I COULD OFFER Ambrose and Sharon for supper Monday evening were grilled cheese sandwiches and tomato soup. Mister Tibbs showed interest in both and migrated between Sharon and Ambrose's feet. Since Sharon liked dogs the least, he spent more time with her.

"How about a beer, Mel?" Ambrose asked.

Sharon shook her head. "I'm glad we could get your car, but it's so much bigger than mine. Unless you're more wiped out than I am, I'd like you to drive. Just be our luck that you'd get pulled over."

Ambrose frowned slightly and looked at Sharon. "I suppose. Does Mel's friend know you drove his car down here?"

"I called the paper and left a message about where I left it."

He looked at me. "That blonde reporter's bugged you before. How'd you keep her from coming over here to look for me?"

"I told them you had cows to milk, so you'd probably be in a rush."

Sharon laughed. "She bought that?"

"She lives in a city. She probably thinks farmers still sit on an overturned bucket and milk by hand."

Ambrose met my eyes. "I bet I wouldn't have been arrested if anybody but Granger had walked into the barn."

Sharon put down her spoon. "Maybe. But when that prosecutor gave his list of reasons, it really shook me up. The sheriff and the county attorney really think you did it."

"I expect they wouldn't have done the whole arrest and court thing if they didn't," Ambrose said.

"At least they did the hearing when you got to town instead of making you spend the night in jail." I turned to Sharon. "How'd you get $5,000 as your part of the bail money on such short notice?"

"I brought the last statement of my teacher's retirement account with me. When we were at the jail, I let Jack Spence, the bondsman, watch me do an Internet fund transfer to my checking account."

"So he basically took a post-dated check?" I asked.

"He's friends with my lawyer and Ken Brownberg," Ambrose said.

"Plus, if my check doesn't clear day after tomorrow, he reports that to the court and they revoke bail." She pointed her spoon at Ambrose. "I need to put it back within sixty days or pay a penalty. Hurry up and prove your innocence."

Though she said the last part with an attempt at a teasing tone, Ambrose shook his head. "I can't begin to think what else to tell them."

I looked at both of them. "I've been talking to a few people."

"Don't," they said together.

"Ambrose, it's not like the movies where your attorney hires an investigator to prove you're innocent. Or if she does, you pay for it and it's expensive."

Sharon said, "There's a killer out there."

Ambrose added, "And you work by yourself in some lonely places."

I pointed my half-eaten sandwich at them. "The thing is, Frost's murder probably wasn't planned. Whoever killed him isn't some bad-ass gang-banger looking to kill again."

"Unless they get scared," Sharon said, quietly.

"Maybe." I explained why someone could have been using the barn to store fireworks. "Maybe Frost saw someone hanging out on the property that morning and went over to tell them to high-tail it out of there."

"That's a stretch," Ambrose said. "He never acted like the caring neighbor type."

"I'm not going back there. I'm just going to ask around. What's the harm in that?"

AFTER FORTY-FIVE MINUTES of tossing in bed, I sat up and turned on a bedside lamp. Mister Tibbs' head popped up before I slid my feet onto the floor.

"Come on, girl, you get a short walk. Just to the truck."

I would bring in Hal's manuscript. Surely his self-indulgent prose would put me to sleep.

My sleeping pants were thread-bare sweats, but that and my tee-shirt would be sufficient for a walk to the truck. Life wasn't a fashion show, and clouds hid the moon.

I grabbed Mister Tibbs' leash before heading out. It would be like her to spot a raccoon and take off in the dark.

We were a few feet from the truck when I heard the shuffling noise. Mister Tibbs sat down and would not budge when I gave her leash a gentle tug.

The metallic sound of the truck door shutting reached me. Someone was nearby!

Without thinking, I yelled, "Hey. Get out of there!"

A low voice said something brief, and someone began running toward the street. Very fast. So fast and in such dark clothes that I couldn't discern whether it was a man or woman.

I didn't want to let go of Mister Tibbs' leash, so she and I walked quickly to the truck rather than run after the burglar. Broken window glass littered the ground by the passenger door.

"Damn it." I leaned down to pick up Mister Tibbs. "It's okay, girl. Back inside. I don't want cut paws for you."

She let me carry her to the foot of the steps leading to my apartment, but insisted on getting down to water the base of the handrail before I took her up.

I stood in the doorway looking toward the side yard where my truck sat. I needed to check the truck. I didn't think anyone would hurt me. The runner had probably been more scared than I was.

Still...

The clock said eleven-forty five. Ryan would be up. I wasn't a dainty ingénue, but I also wasn't a fool.

He picked up on the second ring. "Mel? You okay?"

I told him what had happened. "I want to tape some cardboard over the window, but maybe it's better not to do it alone."

"Be right there."

After enticing Mister Tibbs back to her blanket with a dog biscuit, I took packing tape from a kitchen drawer. The recycling tub in the kitchen corner yielded a slim cardboard box that had held a twenty-four pack of water.

I looked out the window again, peering at every bush visible from my upstairs window. The inky blackness looked sinister, not at all like the typically peaceful River's Edge night.

I waited until Ryan pulled into the driveway before I went back downstairs.

We inspected the damage and got to work. Within ten minutes, I'd put any glass I could find in a plastic bucket I'd brought down.

Ryan almost had the window sealed. He picked up a couple of the now glass-free papers and fanned them. "Who would read Hal's stuff?"

"Probably not what they wanted, but it was in plain sight."

Ryan cut off one more piece of tape and plastered it on a corner of the window. "Have you read it?"

"I couldn't sleep, came down to get it."

Ryan chuckled, softly. "Hal's writing would put anyone to sleep."

"So, Ryan, anything you can tell me about tomorrow's article?"

He frowned. "I thought Scott talked to you about, uh, interacting."

"I'm not trying to sway you, I just want a heads up about what you've already written."

After several seconds, Ryan spoke. "If you aren't calling the police, guess I'll get home." He turned and walked back to his car.

Surprised that he wouldn't talk to me about the article, I watched Ryan back out of the driveway. I walked back to the truck to open the driver's side door, feeling more irritated with each step.

Hal's unfastened manuscript littered the floor or had fallen behind the driver's seat. The thief must have had it in his or her hand when I called to them, and they had jumped like someone had poured water down their shirt on April Fool's Day.

As I gathered the papers, I considered whether the unfinished book was the true target of the burglar, or if it was just someone breaking into a vehicle to pay for a heroin fix. My truck was parked well off the street, and Mrs. Keyser had no side yard light. Still, I'd parked there for almost two years and not been broken into.

When I got back to the apartment, Mister Tibbs had placed herself so close to the apartment door that I had to move her aside with one foot. "It's okay, girl. I'm fine." I shut the door. "And so are you."

I filled a glass of water for myself and put a small amount in Mister Tibbs' bowl. The adrenalin had worn off, and I felt sleepier by the moment. But after all that had happened tonight, I wanted to read some more of Hal's story. That was the start of figuring out if a thief wanted the manuscript.

The four pages I'd read were background about "Lake Ridge," Iowa and its fabulous newspaper. By Chapter Two, Hal's was the tale of local hog farmers, Mattie and Adam Durkins, who had left town to attend a pot-luck-supper with a group of longtime friends.

Sleet had just started, so the roads were getting slick. "Nothing an Iowa farmer can't handle," according to Hal.

For some reason that "would be forever unknown," Mr. Durkins' car had strayed across the two-lane road directly into the path of a semi.

I shivered at his description of a blazing fire that made it almost impossible to discern whether Mr. Durkins had a heart attack or simply misjudged speed on a slick road.

Hal then diverted to one of his pet soap boxes. He had written at least one editorial a year about how local roads, though supposedly banked and maintained for vehicles traveling fifty-five miles per hour, had not been built to accommodate the tractor trailers that carried huge quantities of animal feed or hauled hogs to a meat packing plant.

Hal disguised the opinion as part of a press release from the local sheriff, who lamented the death of the popular farming couple.

I shut my eyes momentarily, trying not to remember photos of my parents' mangled and burned car. Dr. MacGregor identified them because of my father's artificial knee.

Even my mother's dentures had been destroyed in the fire. Since they were known to be attending the pot luck together, no one tried to say Dad's passenger could have been anyone else.

The one solace that night was that I hadn't been on call for the paper. I never had to visit the accident scene.

My indignation mounted. How could Hal use my parents' death as a plot point in a badly written mystery? Or at least what appeared to be shaping up as a mystery.

The book speculated that brake lines had been cut, and intrepid publisher Harry Muldoon searched for a motive for murder.

My stomach clenched. Hal created a motivation in the form of Arthur Springer, who wanted to buy the Durkins' land for a rock-bottom price. From Frost to Springer? Hal had never been subtle.

The rather dull progression from motive to investigation went on for several pages. I yawned and resolved to put the book down at the end of the third chapter.

If Hal had not mentioned interviewing Mr. Springer, I would have happily not read the rest of the manuscript. However, the 'fictional' Springer had reacted with rage at the suggestion that he had something to do with a murder. Harry Muldoon had to "hightail it out of the guy's house before he swung a poker at me."

I put the book aside and picked up the notepad that always rested on my bedside table. I needed to find out if Hal interviewed Peter Frost and whether Hal talked about the book's story line to anyone.

As far as I knew, if Shirley had not run into Hal at an Ottumwa bookstore, no one would have known Hal was writing a book. Unless he interviewed them.

And even if Peter Frost had thought Hal's ideas were in a draft book, what might have taken Frost to the marina to look for it on Hal's old boat? Had he searched Hal's house, too?

I remembered Sandi's and my conversation about Hal's house after his death. Since he never had anyone over, no one could have discerned that something had been stolen.

Then it hit me. Probate! There had been a listing of Hal's assets in the paper roughly ten days ago. He had no will or known heirs, so the lawyer handling the estate wanted nearly all assets listed in the local paper.

Peter Frost learned Hal had a boat and went there to look for Hal's book. Was it because he didn't want the embarrassment of ridiculous speculation about my parents' deaths or to cover up two murders?

CHAPTER ELEVEN

TUESDAY MORNING I AWOKE from a dream about putting together a jigsaw puzzle. I couldn't finish it because Mister Tibbs had chewed several pieces.

After Mister Tibbs and I finished her morning ablutions, I realized I needed to talk to Mrs. Keyser about the broken window. I stood next to the truck and called my car insurance company and South County Glass to arrange to have a new window put in the pickup.

I turned toward her house after the second call and was surprised to see her six inches from me.

"Melanie, I'm not happy about this."

I thought fast. I did not intend to apologize for the broken window, but I couldn't alienate her. "I don't think it says anything about your yard being unsafe. It was just some random idiot looking for change or expensive sunglasses to sell."

She took a step back, now worried instead of accusing. "I never hesitate to go out at night. You think I should?"

"I bet the person didn't expect Mister Tibbs and me to come down. He won't be back."

She sighed. "I suppose the repair people will be here soon."

"No worries there. The glass company will put in the new window while my car's parked at the diner. That way I can be in town to do other things if it takes a while."

Given her knitted brow, Mrs. Keyser had expected to be more in the know if the repair were done in her driveway. She shrugged. "If that's what you think is best, dear."

As Mrs. Keyser walked back into her house, I called Sandi. She might have thoughts about who broke my truck window. She would definitely have an opinion about Hal's book. To me, every page read like a story based on my parents' death. Maybe Sandi would see it differently.

Sandi didn't answer, so I left her a voice message.

I took the cardboard off the truck window and drove to the diner for breakfast. That's when I read the *South County News's* special edition. No wonder Sandi didn't answer her phone.

The article put thoughts of the manuscript and Frost's seeming desire for it out of my mind.

Former Resident Accused of Murder

Ambrose Perkins, disputed owner of land on County Road 270, was arraigned for the murder of Peter Frost, owner of the adjoining farm, with whom he had been in a property dispute.

In a bail hearing yesterday evening, County Attorney Smith cited Perkins' prior threats against Frost as an important factor in the decision to charge him.

I understood what seeing red meant.

Ambrose and I were not disputed owners of our parents' farm. Peter Frost was a bully willing to make fraudulent claims.

The next paragraph opened with Patrick Brannon's statement about Ambrose saying "nothing bad enough" could happen to Frost.

There were a couple more paragraphs, the last of which almost lauded the sheriff for the arrest. Nothing Charlotte Dickey said about Ambrose's lack of motive or anything similar was mentioned.

What made me even angrier than the frowning picture of Ambrose was that the paper had filled extra space with advertising. The four-page special edition made money on Frost's death and Ambrose's wrong arrest.

Railing at Sandi or Ryan would do no good. The sentence structure was more formal than theirs, so I knew Holmes had edited whatever they gave him. Since neither one had called to warn me of the article's tone – I would say bias – I wasn't about to call them.

Instead, I placed a tip for Shirley on the booth's table and stood to leave the diner. Despite my promise to Ambrose to limit my questions, I now planned to rattle some chains.

I WALKED TO THE HARDWARE store while the technician worked on my truck. As Andy waited on another customer, I looked at the Fourth of July items. I could have bought anything from an oven mitt to a child's catcher's mitt in red, white, and blue.

The other customer left, and Andy approached me with the mournful stare of a wet dog. "Sorry about Ambrose."

I was emphatic. "He didn't do it."

Andy nodded, but didn't overtly agree.

I glanced around the front of the store. "I thought you sold sparklers and snakes." I'd always liked the black disks, no bigger than a dime, that rose into the form of a snake when lit.

"Not selling as well as usual, so boss moved 'em to the side aisle." Andy pointed. "He wanted front space for garden hoses and sprinklers."

I walked to the designated aisle and pretended to peruse the two shelves.

Andy trailed after me. "You lookin' for something specific?"

Without regarding him, I said, "I'd like to light a cherry bomb under a couple people's cars, but you don't sell them." I looked at him and smiled. "Probably just as well."

Andy frowned and seemed to ponder something. "You're done at the paper, right?"

"One-hundred percent."

"I might…I mean, I can't be for sure. I might know some people selling that kind of stuff. You know, like reporters say, off the record." He added, "Except you aren't a reporter."

I frowned lightly, as if considering this for several seconds, and fingered a pack of sparklers. "I really wouldn't hurt anybody's car, but I might like to make some noise outside some windows."

"Okay."

When he didn't say more, I asked, "You going to tell me who to call?"

"Since you're not a regular customer, I better have them call you."

Them? Who were they?

"I guess that's fair." I decided to appear uncertain. "You can… Hey, how do I know you won't tell the sheriff?"

He shook his head. "Never happen."

I stifled a smile. Andy wouldn't want Gallagher to know he knew where to get illegal fireworks. "Okay. You've got my numbers from orders I've placed, right?"

I began to walk to the cash register with the sparklers and a package of snakes.

Andy followed me. "Only, you can't tell where you found out."

BY THE TIME I retrieved my truck, visited a few more businesses in town, and stopped by a nursery near Keosauqua – Andy having forgotten to ask about larger pots – I needed a break.

The streets were packed with parked cars, so I parked a block down and strode toward Mason's Diner. Several people walked quickly to their cars, and I figured out why cars lined the street too late to get back into my truck.

The Methodist Church two blocks away must have been where Granger held Peter Frost's funeral. The funeral procession rounded the corner, heading toward me. I wasn't aware that Frost had many friends, but remembered attendees would likely be mostly his nephew's friends.

I thought I would attract more attention by walking away, so I stood back from the curb, across from the diner. I tried to blend in with the gray-frame former flower shop behind me.

The hearse had almost passed me, en route to the town's cemetery, when the window of the limousine behind it rolled down. Aaron Granger was flushed and furious. "You!"

I was too taken aback to respond.

He leaned his head out of the window, but a hand on Granger's shoulder gently pulled him back into the car. The tinted window began to rise, and within a few seconds, the limo turned the corner into the town square.

My knees, which I'd been holding very straight, felt weak. I leaned against the boarded windows of the frame building. I felt as if passengers in every car stared at me, but I knew a lot of them didn't know me.

The final car was the *South County News's* Ford Focus. It slowed, and Sandi jumped out so fast that Ryan barely stopped.

She stared at me. "Are you nuts?"

"I had no idea that procession would come by now. I'm going into the diner."

She took in my stony expression, and flushed. "I didn't write it, you know."

"I know. I'm pissed, but not at you guys."

When she looked away, something clicked, and I stared at her. "Ryan wrote it."

She gestured to the diner without responding. "Come on. The tavern's not open yet. I need at least coffee."

We crossed the street in silence, and I opened the glass door so Sandi could precede me. She had on high heels, not her usual shoes of choice. They clicked and clacked on the tiles as she walked toward a back booth.

Shirley, who had been serving at the counter, looked up. "The usual, girls?"

We both said, "Coffee." I added a thanks.

Sandi slid in across from me. She looked miserable, or at least that's how I interpreted her sagging shoulders and lack of smile.

"The story was accurate, but I wouldn't have slanted it that way."

No way would I let go of my irritation at the paper. "Some of that slant looked like jumping to conclusions to me. And you didn't even include a statement from Ambrose's attorney."

"Mel, if I wanted to sugar coat it, I'd nod. But you're my friend, so I won't."

"You really think Ambrose did it?"

"I know your brother, so no. But I get how it looks like he did."

Shirley neared us, carrying two steaming mugs of coffee, so I said only, "I suppose."

"You suppose what, Sugar?" She set the mugs in front of us and made no effort to move.

I ignored her question. I had my own. "You remember that time you were in Ottumwa at the bookstore and saw Hal?"

Shirley narrowed her eyes and raised an eyebrow as she looked down at me. "I said I saw Hal, not Ambrose."

I smiled. "I know. Turns out, he was writing some kind of book. He left it in his boat."

"I knew it! About River's Edge? He gave me the creeps. Who'd he out?"

"Out?" Sandi asked. "Nobody's afraid to say they're gay anymore."

Shirley dismissed the idea with a hand wave. "Not that. I always figured he had the goods on somebody."

"He was always looking," I agreed. "I only read the first few pages so far. What do you think he was writing about?"

"When I talked to him, you know, when he came in here, he only said it was a murder mystery that would rock people's socks."

Sandi snorted. "Ever the jackass."

Shirley was not to be diverted. "How's Ambrose?"

"He's home. You know anybody who hated Peter Frost?"

"He wasn't too popular. Mostly folks was mad about him trying to grab your parents' place."

I knew that. I wanted something different. "Ever hear him say anything about telling people to get off my farm?"

"He didn't come in here much. Hadn't seen him for a couple weeks." The front door opened, and she turned to glance at three women who were dressed as if en route to church. "Be right with you. Grab any booth."

She looked back at me. "Two or three times a month, he'd be in here with his Granger nephew. 'Bout ten days ago he sat with Mr. Jackson from the bank."

"I wonder what they talked about?"

She turned to walk to the customers. "You find out, you pass it on."

I looked at Sandi. "I heard he might be having financial troubles."

She shrugged. "Could've just been refinancing. No one at the bank will talk to me about something like that."

"I'll ask around."

Sandi downed half her cup of coffee and licked her lips. "I needed a jolt. I think your best bet is getting more focus on his time of death."

I avoided saying Frost's time of death was the crux of the entire problem.

She seemed to take my silence as disagreement. "Look, Mel, your barn wasn't too hot. Frost's body temp was almost ninety-eight point six. That likely means somebody killed him fairly soon before you guys got there. Emphasis on somebody, not necessarily Ambrose."

"But if it comes to a trial, Ambrose will have had to sell everything he owns to pay legal bills."

"So dig more."

"What else do you know?"

She leaned toward me. "And you didn't hear from me that the Donovans saw more cars on the road than usual. After dark."

"Huh. And it's not really dark 'til nine. By then there's hardly anyone on the roads out there." I thought in silence for perhaps fifteen seconds.

"Melanie." Sandi's tone was half amused, half strident. "You haven't asked me anything about Peter Frost's funeral."

"Gee, I didn't, did I? All I'm thinking about is Ambrose."

Sandi frowned as she nodded. "You know how funerals are, no one ever gets up and says the dead person was an SOB or had an affair with someone's wife."

"So, no good info?"

"He never married, and it seems he has no relatives except Aaron Granger. And he looked pretty broken up."

"Granger's mother was Frost's sister?" I asked.

Her brow furrowed. "Odd, but no one discussed her. Did you read the obit in yesterday's paper? It said Frost and Granger's mom grew up in Kirksville, Missouri."

"Gee, I only read the article, not the obit."

"It was short. He farmed all his life, but mostly in Missouri. You know Frost hadn't lived here that long. I had the impression from the funeral home, you know, from talking to the funeral home after they emailed us the obit, that Frost moved here to be near Granger."

"Jeez." I did feel bad if Granger and Frost were each other's only kin, but I couldn't get too broken up. Ambrose could go to trial for Frost's murder. Even if he were acquitted, he'd be ruined financially and probably emotionally.

"What are you going to do?" Sandi asked.

I raised both eyebrows. "I thought you weren't allowed to talk to me about the story."

She shrugged, and her smile was grim. "I'm not. I never said I wouldn't use your leads to write."

"Not funny."

"I didn't mean it to be. I'll talk to you whenever you want, but not on the phone or via email. We can meet at Hy-Vee or something." She thought for a moment. "I can call you from Betty's phone. She leaves her mobile on her desk at the paper all the time."

"Ridiculous," I murmured.

"Best I can do. And I am noticing that you aren't telling me what you're doing."

CHAPTER TWELVE

I STILL HAD TO MAKE a living, but instead of driving home or marketing my planter idea to more local businesses, I went to the bank. No one would talk to me about Peter Frost directly, so I'd open a new account and chat with staff as they helped me.

First Bank of Southeast Iowa only has two branches, one in River's Edge and one in Keosauqua. Ours is so small it doesn't warrant safe deposit boxes. Still, without it I'd do more driving.

The whoosh of cold air as I opened the door almost startled me. The two tellers had on sweaters.

I waved to them and went to the seating area outside the two cubicles that are today's version of offices. The assistant manager would see me when she got off the phone.

Sure enough, within ten seconds Melissa Martin, a classmate of Ambrose's, smiled and held up her index finger to acknowledge that she had seen me. I nodded to her.

No other customers were in the bank, and I watched the two tellers pull out their phones to show one another recent pictures they had taken. I longed to have nothing more to think about than sharing photos.

Melissa interrupted my thoughts. "Melanie? May I help you?"

I stood and held out a hand. She took it in her beautifully manicured one, and I said, "I need to open a second checking account, for my yard work and landscaping business."

She gestured that I should precede her into the cubicle, and I sat in a chair opposite her desk. The predominant decorating colors were mauve and tan. Melissa's sweater matched the mauve.

She began a practiced pitch. In less than a minute, I knew there were several kinds of checking accounts, and I could not avoid a monthly fee.

Our eyes met as she ended the spiel, and Melissa looked away and then back. "I'm sorry about Ambrose's arrest."

I tried not to sound strident. "He didn't do it."

She nodded and turned to her computer to enter information from my driver's license.

"So, Melissa, did you know Peter Frost?"

She put my license closer to her eyes to read the tiny letters. "Not outside of the bank. He did come in pretty regularly."

That surprised me. With the ubiquity of ATM machines and debit cards, most people rarely walked into a bank. "Maybe he liked your free coffee."

She grinned briefly as she typed. "He always had a cup. Lately he seemed more relaxed."

Melissa began sending documents to the printer.

When she didn't appear ready to volunteer more, I said, "He was my parents' neighbor for years, but they didn't speak all that often. My dad thought Frost was bitter, because he paid more for his land than it's worth now."

She smiled. "It's all about the price of corn, isn't it?"

I nodded. "I heard he was going to look for part-time work." *Liar, liar.*

She frowned slightly. "He may have found something. He started making cash deposits regularly."

Her expression took on a look of panic, and she spoke fast. "Oh my. I guess because he's not a customer now, I mean he's dead, I was chatting, not banking."

Aloud, I said, "No worries."

Internally I yelled, "Bingo!"

Melissa gave only perfunctory replies over the next few minutes and seemed relieved when I signed papers, ordered checks, and left.

I didn't care what kind of deposits Frost made, it was more that the cash seemed to be something new. People tended to deposit cash after a rummage sale or if they were trying to hide income from the IRS.

Did Frost make money under the table? And was it an activity that got him killed?

I nearly ran into Ryan as I left the bank. We stood in awkward silence, the *South County News's* very anti-Ambrose article hanging between us.

I couldn't avoid the topic. "Why, Ryan?"

He stared at me for a couple seconds. "He was next to the body, and he had the knife in his hand."

My neck went back, chin went down, and eyebrows up, an expression that I hoped said either "is that all" or maybe "you've got to be kidding me."

His chin jutted out, his expression of stubbornness. "I had to go with the evidence."

I spoke with contempt. "You showed no 'evidence' to counter Ambrose's explanation. I think you went with what your boss wanted. You can't do that if you get to a big daily."

He flushed and turned again toward his car. "I'll catch you later."

BY ONE O'CLOCK, Nelson had called. Without referring to Andy, he said that he and his cousin could "help me out, but not 'til after dark."

Nelson and Harlan didn't scare me in daylight or dark, but that didn't mean I would meet them in a poorly lit part of town. I suggested we meet in the parking lot at the softball fields. Practice for the Fourth of July games would be ending, so at least some people would be around.

I drove to the nursery near Keosauqua to pick up the large planting containers and ten bags of soil they had ordered for me yesterday. As I came back into town from the north, my cell phone rang.

"How about Plants and Pots?" Stooper asked.

It took me a second to realize he had suggested a name for my (our?) business. "That's the best they could come up with at the diner?"

"Shirley wanted The Green Thumb."

"I think maybe we need something that shows we do landscaping work." I pulled into the driveway of my apartment. "What about Clear and Plant?"

"Huh. Could work. Lemme think more. You comin' by Syl's?"

"I have to walk Mister Tibbs. You need me at Syl's, or are you up for helping me put out a few large planters at businesses on the square?"

"Come by with your lady and look at how I put the roses on the trellises." He hung up.

Stooper worked hard, but he didn't dwell on the niceties of dealing with people.

I opened the door to my apartment and Mister Tibbs rocketed out. She almost knocked me into the railing. Before I could call to her, she had reached the bottom of the stairs and begun to pee with great vigor.

I leaned into the apartment and grabbed her leash from a peg by the door. By the time I got to her she had finished and hung her head.

"You're a good girl. I'm sorry. I didn't know I gave you too much water." I patted her head, and we trotted around the back yard at a fast clip, with me holding the leash rather than fastening it.

I rarely worried that she would run away. Mister Tibbs was a mess when I found her in Syl's small barn, and she now didn't want to be too far from the person who fed her. Unless she found a varmint to chase.

I looked down at her. "We're going to Syl's. You can stay down here while I do my business and lock the door." I dropped her leash on the ground and walked upstairs.

When I got to the bathroom, I found splashes of water around the toilet. No wonder her bladder was full. Apparently she had learned how to stand on her hind legs to lap water. "Ugh."

I grabbed a couple of granola bars from a kitchen cupboard and went back outside. Mister Tibbs greeted me, by slobbering on my calf, and trotted behind me to the pickup.

When she settled on her blanket on the back seat, I backed out of the driveway and headed to Syl's. "If you decide to poop at Syl's place, make sure you do it in a flower garden or by the barn."

When we got to Syl's, Stooper had just pulled the riding mower into the barn. Mister Tibbs and I parked and walked to the white trellises.

A quick look at the roses told me Stooper's hands probably bore a lot of scratches. He doesn't like to be bothered with gloves.

Stooper called from behind me. "Hey, Mel. Even enough, you think?"

"They look great. I'm surprised you got the trellises to stand so straight."

He pointed to a spot near the fence. "I tied 'em with white string for now. I'll pack 'em better into the ground over the next few months."

"Good idea." I looked down. Mister Tibbs stood on her hind feet, looking at Stooper with an expectant expression. "Mister Tibbs. Leave him alone."

Stooper flushed. "I been keeping a dog treat in my pocket now and again."

"You're such a sucker."

He grinned and held out a mini milk bone. "Mostly for her."

"So, I have a bunch of big flower pots in the truck and some bags of topsoil. I figure we can put a couple on the square today."

"You got plants?"

"Oh, crud."

He laughed. "Gimme ten bucks, and I'll get some at the hardware store."

I reached in a pocket and took out a bill. "Last time I checked, all I saw were a few geraniums. I should have bought more earlier."

"Some daisies in the back. I saw 'em when I picked up a lawn edger for Syl the other day."

Stooper and Syl have developed what I would call an unexpected friendship. Syl is the well-educated Californian whose data analysis skills are so finely honed that an Iowa insurance association hired him to develop some kind of database.

Stooper is the ultimate nice guy, but he was fortunate to graduate from high school and has always worked with his back. The two men seem to have bonded in part because Stooper's advice to Syl, on taking care of a large lawn in a climate he's unfamiliar with, is valuable. And they both root for the St. Louis Cardinals, although I doubt if Syl did before he met Stooper.

"Hey, Stooper."

He turned from walking toward his car. "You need more than plants?"

"Are you doing a headstone for Peter Frost?"

"Granger had him cremated."

I shuddered. Because our parents had died in a fiery crash, we needed no caskets. Ambrose and I have a stone in the cemetery in their memory.

"You okay?"

"Yep. I've been thinking a lot about the man. We barely knew him, but his death is ruining Ambrose's life."

Stooper shifted his weight from one foot to the other, seeming unsure what to say.

"Sorry. Don't mean to be morbid. If I could just figure out why he went to our place."

"You don't think he was in the fireworks business thing, do you?"

Mister Tibbs had finished chasing squirrels. She plopped her head on my shoe and rolled to one side.

"Hard to think he'd do that with his nephew being a sheriff's deputy."

I thought about the cash deposits and straightened. What if the people storing something in the barn were paying Peter Frost so he wouldn't report them to the sheriff?

WHEN MISTER TIBBS and I got to Mr. Patel's store, I was still thinking about how Peter Frost would have made enough cash to make more regular bank deposits. As far as I knew, he had no carpentry, plumbing skills, or any other talent people would pay cash for if they could get a discount.

Mister Tibbs and I were greeted by a large black cat that I'd never noticed sitting by the door. It posed regally, just to the side of the entry, and either wasn't intimidated by people or scared them off so no one entered the store.

I opened the back of the pickup and took out a large, rust-colored pot and three bags of topsoil.

Mister Tibbs refused to leave the truck. I left the door open so she could watch me work. The cat apparently saw its role as supervisor because it didn't move, even when Mr. Patel walked out.

"I didn't know you had a cat."

"Neither did I. It showed up yesterday." He glanced at the cat. "And I was dumb enough to feed it."

"Maybe an owner will show up. Boy or girl?"

"Either a girl or a snipped boy. I haven't inspected too closely."

A single honk announced Stooper.

I nodded toward his car, and in a lowered voice said, "You can get to know him better."

Stooper unloaded two flats of plants from his front seat, and Mr. Patel walked over to inspect them.

I listened to them exchange pleasantries as I emptied one bag of soil into the pot. Mr. Patel walked back inside, and Stooper insisted on handling the next two bags. I arranged the daisies and geraniums, not the best combination, on the ground so I could decide how to place them in the pot.

"Is this your cat?"

I looked toward the store and saw a girl of maybe ten stooping next to the black cat.

"No, and Mr. Patel isn't sure where it lives, so it's best not to touch it."

A boy of perhaps thirteen or fourteen stood twenty yards down the sidewalk and called, "Come on, Rachel."

She petted the cat and then looked at me. "I like your daisies."

By this time, Mister Tibbs had emerged from my truck. She sat on the sidewalk in front of the store, alternately looking at me, Stooper, Rachel, and the cat.

"Rachel," I said, "is that your brother calling you?"

She looked at me and smiled shyly. "He wants me to keep up."

The brother walked to within a few feet from Rachel. His polite tone was probably more for my benefit than

Rachel's. "Come on, Mom's home and she'll play with you."

With a resigned sigh, Rachel stood and took his hand.

When they were out of earshot, Stooper said, "Bet he loves carting her around."

I thought of how patient Ambrose had been with me and wished that for Rachel.

A vehicle's shadow came over me, and I looked up. David hopped out of his truck and walked to Stooper and me. "You guys need any fertilizer?"

"Phew," Stooper said. "You drive that a lot, you must have some good nose clips."

David grinned. "I don't even smell it anymore."

"How much for three bags?" I asked.

He looked disappointed. "That all you need?"

"For now. Later I'll probably need more for other projects."

"Betterin' none," David said. "I'll unload it."

Stooper didn't offer to help.

I had David put the bags in the back of my pickup. If he'd come a bit earlier, I'd have added some to the middle of the large flower pot. Certainly not on the top.

When the truck pulled away, Stooper said, "I didn't know he sold that stuff."

"Ran into him and Brad at last Sunday's farmers' market. It's cheap because it's not fully aged."

"No shit."

I laughed. "Yes, shit."

CHAPTER THIRTEEN

I GOT TO THE BALL fields about eight-thirty Tuesday evening. Land along the river isn't worth building on. Heck, in twenty years half the softball field could be lost to erosion.

For today and the near future, the park has the softball field, a refreshment stand called the Snack Shack made of recycled plastic from a small plant in Bonaparte, and a large swing set complete with sliding board. Anything on the site could be easily removed during a flood or cleaned afterwards.

I leaned against the chain link fence watching Mike, who runs the McKinney car repair shop in town, try to strike out a muscular guy who looked to be about forty. There were two outs. When the call got to three balls and two strikes, Mike relaxed for what he probably thought would be a final pitch.

Brad Thomas came to the plate. I hoped he didn't smell like his organic fertilizer. His bat cracked on the first pitch, and the grounded double let in two more runs.

From the bench that held Chamber of Commerce and Rotary members came a collective groan. The military service veterans appeared to be on track for their fifth straight July Fourth win.

Apparently the umpire wanted to go home. He waved his hands above his head in a crisscross motion and yelled, "Called because of dark." The two teams probably could have gone another inning, but it would likely have been painful to watch.

I glanced around, still not seeing Nelson or his cousin. A Dr. Pepper was in order, and I got to the Snack Shack in time to hear Shirley yell, "Last call. Get your butts over here if you want a drink."

I grinned and took a dollar bill out of my pocket. "Hey, Shirley. Doing double duty?"

She flashed a smile and pulled a Dr. Pepper from a metal tub on the counter. Ice cold, the way she knew I liked it.

"Hey, Shug. Just for the Fourth. Haven't seen you here since Hal got kicked out a couple years ago."

I put the bill on the counter and took the can. "He said he'd fire us if we hung out here during practice. At the time, I liked my job."

She shook her head. "Old Hal." She took remaining cans of soda from the tub, and I lifted it off the counter to dump the ice water a few feet from the shack.

A car horn beeped in the nearby lot. When I looked, a hand came from the window and waved at me. I put the tub back and walked to the beat-up, gray Chevy Taurus.

Nelson stepped out of the car. "Kind of a busy place."

"I can pay you now and meet you later for the stuff."

He nodded. "Hardware store parking lot is good."

Harlan sat in the passenger seat, but ignored us. From his posture, it seemed he was scanning the Internet on his mobile phone.

"I don't want to buy a lot, but thought it would be fun for a couple friends and me to have our own show. Maybe after the town fireworks."

"Best time." Nelson pulled a rumpled sheet of paper from the breast pocket of a stained denim shirt. "Half the town's doing it then, so cops only pay attention if you set 'em off in the street."

"Good advice. I want some fountains and a few Roman candles." My dad would light off the conical fountains that spewed sparks fifteen or more feet into the air.

"I got the fountains, but not the candles." He named a ridiculously high price.

"Gee, I had no idea it would be that expensive."

Nelson's eye roll and expression implied I was an idiot. "See, we have transportation and security costs. Or you could go to Missouri yourself and get 'em."

I thought quickly. I wanted to find out if he'd had Roman candles earlier and sold out, or if he still had them and was keeping them for someone. "I'm happy to get them from you. Wish you had the candles, though."

"We had some last year, but they cost too much this year. If we got stuck with even a few it'd cut into profits."

I suppressed a smile as we agreed on the quantity, and I forked over the money. The Nelson I knew never talked like a business man before. "You know where I can get any?"

Nelson frowned. "I heard somebody else is selling this year, but I'm not gonna send you to the competition."

Now I did grin. "Aren't you the entrepreneur?"

Harlan's strident voice came from inside the car. "We gotta go, Nelson."

I nodded to Harlan, and to Nelson said, "I'm usually in town. Just let me know when to meet you at the store."

They pulled out, and I walked to my truck, thinking. Another person might be selling in town, or it could have been Nelson's way of blowing me off. If he and Harlan had been using the barn, they might not want to own up to having the candles. They wouldn't want me to know who shot them at me.

Before today, I hadn't thought of Nelson as organized enough to gather eggs in a hen house, much less run a business and use my parents' barn as some sort of distribution point for illegal goods. Perhaps I should change that thinking.

I CALLED AMBROSE Wednesday to see how he was doing.

"I was so damn nervous about staying in jail, I spent yesterday feeling relieved. Worked in the beans all day."

"Who would've thought farming in the hot sun would be relaxing?"

Ambrose's laugh was one of sarcasm. "Today, I'm getting mad again. At the sheriff and, now, that reporter friend of yours."

"I'm not sure I feel too friendly toward Ryan just now."

Ambrose paused. "Maybe when he finds out how wrong he was, it'll teach him a lesson."

I didn't want to talk about Ryan. "You going down to the Dubuque sheriff to check in?"

"Yeah. I know him from Farm Bureau. He called last night to say he talked to Gallagher. I'm 'sposed to stop by anytime except lunch."

I had to laugh. "I don't think they'd be like this in New York City."

"Or Des Moines. Listen, I have a telephone appointment to go over a lot of stuff with Ms. Dickey, that's what she said to call her, day after the Fourth. You think of anything she should know?"

I said nothing for a few seconds. "I've found out that Nelson and his cousin for sure sell fireworks, but somehow I can't believe they'd be smart enough to distribute a bunch of them from our barn."

"Uh, Mel, I meant anything you might think of from that day. Let's leave any poking around to Ms. Dickey."

I tried not to sound aggravated. Ambrose needed to get more involved in figuring out what happened to Peter Frost. "What about the autopsy report? Will she have it?

"Mel, stay out of any investigating."

I made no commitment. "How come you're not talking until the fifth?"

"She had some plans set up. We need a break, too. Sharon's a lot more upset than I am. We're going to barbeque on the Fourth and invite a couple friends over."

"Since you can't leave your farm except to talk to your sheriff?"

He gave a short laugh. "I'm allowed to go to church. Maybe I'll take it up again."

After we hung up, I outlined my day. I'd go back to our barn. If someone had been using it, maybe tire tracks would show behind it. Or maybe there had been tracks, and the sheriff's crew had already sampled them. How would I find that out?

I headed first to the hospital to see what I could learn from the autopsy report. Dr. James T. MacGregor, Jr., is head of Pathology and Hematology and also serves as South County's medical examiner. He had talked to me about Hal's autopsy, even though he hadn't performed it. Why not Peter Frost's?

The old tile hallway outside his hospital office had been polished to a high sheen. Idly, I wondered if the hospital got business from people who slipped on it.

Dr. MacGregor saw me right away, possibly to avoid my talking to his staff.

I sat across from him in a chair with a leather seat and back and wooden arms. The formal chairs matched the doctor's arrow-straight posture. He started talking before I could ask any questions.

"You'll read articles that say a deceased person's body temperature declines one-and-a-half degrees per hour, but there really isn't an exact standard." He focused on a pen as he twirled it and didn't look at me. "You probably watch crime shows where killers think freezing a body will throw off an investigation. It can. Same thing with excess heat."

"So, did something make Mr. Frost's temperature so close to normal? For a dead person, I mean?"

He sighed. "The barn was almost the perfect environment for using temperature as a guide. Not too hot, not too cold. I was out of town, so I didn't go to the site, but another doctor rushed out there." He met my gaze. "Rectally, that's the most accurate measurement."

I felt my face shift into a grimace. "But you did the final report. Something must've led you to think he died right before Ambrose got there."

In an almost gentle tone, he said, "Largely temperature."

I thought for several seconds. "I, uh, didn't see a lot of blood."

"Frankly, if the blade hadn't nicked his aortic valve, he probably would have lived. If the killer had, uh, not done anything else."

"So why didn't I see much blood?"

"Largely internal bleeding."

"So the knife did a lot of damage?"

"As I said, if he had received prompt treatment... It was the most common type of aortic tear, which occurs in the ascending aorta, the beginning of the vessel where it emerges from the top of the heart." He patted his heart with his left hand. "It's a big enough segment that it could be hard to miss with a knife to the shoulder."

"Huh. Fast or slow?" I asked.

Dr. McGregor shifted in his chair. "It shouldn't have taken too long."

"But could it? I mean, if he didn't move around, he wouldn't have bled really fast, would he? Maybe someone stabbed him and then called Ambrose."

Dr. McGregor stood. "Melanie, I hope Ambrose is cleared of this crime. All I can do is report my findings." He held out his hand to shake. "His lawyer was sent the autopsy report the morning after the hearing."

Knowing it wouldn't do any good to press, I accepted the handshake and thanked him.

I drove to the library, thinking I'd print some articles on things like internal bleeding and body temperature. After sitting in front of the building for almost two minutes, I drove away.

Ms. Dickey had to have staff who would look into that. I lived in River's Edge, able to talk to people. Someone in this town had either killed Peter Frost or knew who did.

CHAPTER FOURTEEN

EVERYTHING BEGAN WITH THE barn, so I drove back to the farm. Neglect was becoming more apparent. In late March, after the month roared out as a lion, I'd had some shingles replaced. They gleamed light gray against the much darker older ones.

Around the side steps, tall dandelions were ready to spread to the rest of the yard. They were almost as tall as a pile of flagstones my father had planned to place near the back porch.

In prior years I'd asked the people who mowed the lawn to put down some weed killer. Since I had a few weeks of unemployment earlier this year, I hadn't done that yet. I had meant to ask Ambrose to take care of it, but kept forgetting.

I had a quick image of my father's face as he picked me up off the short sidewalk after I skinned my knee when I was about six. Tears prickled, and I looked to the barn. I needed to focus on it.

The pickup sat in the hot sun, so I put down the windows before I got out to walk around the barn.

There were a bunch of broken stalks of corn behind the building, but sheriff's deputies clomping around could have done that. The leaves on the stalks were withered, so they'd been down for at least a few days. The killer could easily have trampled them.

"But no one thought to look," I murmured.

I had hoped to find tire tracks, but the soil hadn't been moist. I saw vestiges of tire marks, but the tracks were broken by footprints and what looked like – maybe – broom marks. Had someone tried to cover vehicle tracks?

I slid open the back barn door and inhaled the stale air. I imagined I smelled the mix of the cows Dad had kept there, tractor oil, and rotting hay. He never let it rot, that was only in the months after his death, before Ambrose and I had it hauled out and shut the barn. Or thought we had shut it.

"None of those things are here," I said. "I want to know about now."

The light Syl had found was gone, and someone had made white circles around all the pieces of Velcro on the walls. I needed to ask Sheriff Gallagher what he made of the lights. Surely it buttressed the idea that someone had been in the barn. A lot.

With the front door closed, the dim light and stuffy air oppressed me. I walked through the barn and slid the front door partly open, reminding myself to get some kind of lock.

For some reason, I usually walked to the left to get to the back of the building. Probably because Dad always did.

Left was closer to the road, right nearer the corn field. For now, I walked right.

Bunches of tire tracks littered the ground, but I remembered that sheriff's cars and the coroner's van had parked on this side of the barn.

I felt so frustrated. No one had cared to hunt for tire tracks or anything else. They were so sure Ambrose had killed Peter Frost.

I circled the barn and then stood facing it, from the back. In irritation, I kicked at the dirt.

I almost missed the thin piece of string. Or was it string? I stooped to pick it up and smelled it. A mild mix of black powder and sulfur emanated from it.

A firecracker fuse, which must have been overlooked as the murderers packed up after they killed Peter Frost. I felt confident in thinking this, but a fuse wouldn't convince Gallagher.

That settled it. I had to make Nelson and Harlan tell me what they knew.

BUT I WOULD HAVE TO find them first. With only 7,500 people, River's Edge isn't too spread out. I drove through downtown and a couple of the more modest neighborhoods. Nelson's car wasn't in sight.

They were supposed to call me to arrange a time to meet at the hardware store for delivery of my fireworks. I didn't feel very patient.

Waiting wouldn't go any faster if I sat in the diner or moped somewhere else, so I headed for the Chamber of Commerce office on the square. I heaved one of the large pots, two bags of topsoil, and some delightfully smelly organic fertilizer from the back of the pickup. It felt good to work.

After about twenty minutes, I realized I still hadn't bought any bedding plants.

I stuck my head inside the office and said I'd be back in a few minutes. Then I drove toward the hardware store. Tomorrow – no ifs, ands, or buts – I'd head to the greenhouse outside of town and buy several flats of annuals.

For a change, good fortune appeared. Before my keys were out of the pickup's ignition, Nelson pulled into the parking spot next to mine.

I walked to his car, and he got out with a white plastic bag that sported the hardware store logo. Smart. Anyone seeing him would think he had something to return.

"So, Mel, make sure you don't leave these in a hot car."

I looked in his car as I took the bag. "No Harlan today?"

Nelson grinned. "He's doing business in another state."

It took me a second to realize he meant Harlan was buying fireworks in Missouri to sell in River's Edge. "Ah, inventory replacement."

Nelson looked momentarily confused, then asked a question of his own. "I heared you told the sheriff you found some black powder in your barn."

I felt like adding "and a fuse," but didn't. "Can't be sure why it was on the floor, but my dad hadn't kept anything like that in the barn for years. Seemed odd."

Nelson got back in his car. I shifted the bag of fireworks to my other hand and looked toward his open driver's side window.

"I appreciate the goods." I hoped he'd say more. When he didn't, I asked, "You have any ideas about how the powder got in the barn?"

"Kind of quiet out there, isn't it?" He stared at his steering wheel, one hand on each side of it. "At your parents' old place. Seems somebody would be noticed, they was in your barn."

If I had scripted comments for him, they would not have been these. Nelson seemed to have signaled that he hadn't been in the barn. Would an innocent man bother to do that? Or maybe he wanted to figure out if our barn was now a good place to stash his illegal products.

"It is quiet. In fact, I'm going to stop by the Donovans' this afternoon to see if they noticed extra traffic near our farm."

Nelson nodded and started his car. "I don't think Ambrose done it."

After he left, I walked into the store feeling confused. Had Nelson tried to say he *knew* Ambrose hadn't killed Peter Frost? Or had he been fishing to see what I thought about the barn and the murder?

As I entered the store, Andy's voice had its usual whine. "Stooper said you might need more plants, so I set a few aside for you."

"Gee, that's really nice. What do I owe you?"

"If you want all of them, fifteen dollars."

I took a twenty dollar bill from the pocket of my jeans and handed it to him.

Rather than ring up the sale, he walked with me toward the back of the store. "I'll point 'em out to you and then give you your change."

The lawn and garden supplies and plants are in a large room with a door that leads to the outside of the hardware store. All seasonal products are kept in it in their turn, so Andy had no need to guide me.

I figured he planned to get five dollars in change from the cash drawer and ring up a sale for less than fifteen dollars. A tidy profit for five minutes' work. More accurately, theft.

The plants showed signs of past dryness, but the now damp soil made me think the plants wouldn't die. I picked up a tray of geraniums, daisies, and a few marigolds that I'd thought were sold out. I'd definitely have to get better plants from the greenhouse.

I stopped at the cash register counter, and Andy handed me a five-dollar bill. "You still plantin' the square?" he asked.

"Doing my best." I began to open the glass exit door with my hip, but turned toward him. "Thanks for letting Nelson know about me."

Andy's brow furrowed. "You hush about that."

I INTENDED TO HEAD to the square, but before I reached it, I pulled over to call Sheriff Gallagher. He took my call. I'd half expected him to tell me he would only talk to Charlotte Dickey.

"Thanks for talking to me. I wondered if there were any fingerprints near where the lights were hung in our barn."

At first I thought he had hung up. Then, he said, "Melanie, now that Ambrose has been arrested, it's a very formal process. A process you are not part of."

"I understand, but…"

"No buts, Melanie. Now, you want to tell me something, you can call. But I won't be passing information to anyone except Ambrose's attorney."

I managed to thank him before I hung up.

I FINISHED PLACING planters in front of the pharmacy and Mason's diner, and then I went home to clean up a bit and tend to Mister Tibbs. She has caught onto my schedule and does not like short visits that are simply to let her potty.

We finished her business and started toward the stairs to the apartment. She strained to go toward the truck.

I stopped. She sat on the ground and thumped her tail expectantly.

I tried to frown at her, but couldn't. "Okay, you can ride in the truck while I visit the Donovans' place."

Her leash was fastened, so I knew she wouldn't wander too far. I ran up the steps, retrieved my purse, and grabbed two bottles of water from the fridge. When I came down, she stood from where she had been lying on cool dirt and began walking to the truck.

I spoke aloud to her as we drove. "How long do you think it took Peter Frost to die? That's the crux of it all. If someone stabbed him at about nine in the morning, maybe he bled internally until right before Ambrose got there."

Mister Tibbs yawned and made a sort of squeaky sound. I turned my head slightly so she and her blanket were in view. She lay on her back with her feet in the air.

"You aren't going to sleep, are you? You wanted to come."

We were nearing our farm, so I slowed and stared as we went by. It looked maddeningly calm. There should be a big sign that said, "Ambrose didn't do it."

I turned into the Donovans' driveway. Their barn was behind the house instead of across from it, so they had a front lawn with shrubs and flower beds. Three beds overflowed with day lilies, daisies, zinnias, petunias, and hostas. I hadn't remembered them as flower people.

I had considered calling, but if they said I couldn't come by there would be no alternative. I'd known the family all my life, though their children were quite a bit older than I. Whenever a neighbor needed help and several families came together, Mrs. Donovan always made a huge vat of mashed potatoes with a lot of butter and milk.

The front door opened as I started up the steps.

Mrs. Donovan looked serious for a couple seconds, and then she broke into a broad smile. It showed perfectly spaced teeth, not what I'd remembered, so probably dentures. "Come in Melanie. I thought we'd see you before now."

I didn't want to say I'd been told she knew nothing, so I smiled and said, "I hated to bother you."

The living room was unexpected. Gone were dated shag carpet and overstuffed furniture. The floor sported blue and white tile, and the walls were a bright yellow. The style imitated magazine-perfect country chic, complete with a replica of an old washstand with a white bowl and pitcher.

"This is beautiful."

Mr. Donovan walked in from the dining room. "Should be. Cost two arms and four legs."

They were in their late seventies or early eighties. I remembered them as a bit overweight, always wearing faded denim complemented by flannel shirts.

Today they were both almost slim, and Mrs. Donovan wore a pale blue shirtwaist with a chunky navy blue necklace. Mr. Donovan had on newly pressed jeans and a collared beige shirt. Neither would make the cover of *Vogue*, but they had been transformed.

When I said nothing, they both laughed. Mr. Donovan said, "We won twenty thousand on a scratch-off ticket."

Mrs. Donovan continued as she gestured to a dark blue armchair, one of two by the window. She took its mate. "All our lives we saved for a rainy day. We decided to spend that money as if it was a sunny day."

"Course, I wouldn't've done pastels," he said, pulling an oak Windsor chair around to face his wife and me.

I sat. "It's lovely."

"Every afternoon, well almost," Mr. Donovan said, "we get out of our farmin' clothes and into something nice."

I smiled. "It suits you."

Mrs. Donovan stopped smiling. "Listen to us go on. You're here because Ambrose is accused of killing that ill-tempered Peter Frost."

"Yes. The sheriff's people said you didn't notice anything that day, but I wondered if you'd seen anything odd in the days preceding his murder."

"Since we know Ambrose would never have done that," she began.

He interrupted, "Unless Frost attacked him first."

Mrs. Donovan leaned toward me. "Don't interrupt dear. We couldn't come up with anything except noticing more traffic sometimes."

"After dark," Mr. Donovan said.

"Mostly," she continued, "we thought people started down the road and realized they'd missed the turn that would get them back to the Henry's place. She's got honey bees now and, oh my, do they make some good honey."

"Lip smackin' good." Mr. Donovan recognized that he'd cut in on his wife's story, and winked at me. "Thing was, it was usually after dark. We thought they were turning around in your folks' driveway."

"But you didn't notice any activity in the barn?" I asked.

They shook their heads, and she added, "Course to really see over that rise, you have to go upstairs. We never had any cause to look."

"And we have that new big-screen TV in what used to be the breakfast room, off the kitchen." Mrs. Donovan nodded sideways toward her husband. "One of us needs it turned up loud."

I sat back in the comfortable chair. "Right after Mr. Frost filed suit against Ambrose and me, he'd stop over at our farm. You probably remember I asked the county attorney to tell him to stay away."

"Far as I know," Mr. Donovan said, "he mostly did. I saw him by the barn 'bout a month ago. Guess he'd walked over. I pulled in. He said he'd seen a green car there, but when he walked up, it left."

"A green car," I mused.

"Now that I think about it," Mr. Donovan added, "I didn't meet it coming toward our place, and I didn't see a lot of dust ahead. You know, heading into town."

Mrs. Donovan frowned. "You mean you think he lied?"

He shrugged. "Can't say. If there was a car, it had headed into town at least two or three minutes before. It was right dry, and no car was kickin' up dust ahead of me."

"Odd that he would walk down there," I murmured. "At his age."

"Pish posh," Mrs. Donovan said. "Ask me how far we walk when we go to the very back field."

I grinned at her. "Point taken." I sobered. "If he walked over there, especially if he stayed off the road, he could've gotten to our farm without being noticed."

"But why?" she asked.

"I keep thinking someone had stuff stored in the barn, maybe entering it through the back after dark. Maybe Frost was, I don't know, checking because he'd seen someone. Or maybe he watched the barn to be sure the sheriff didn't get tipped off."

Mrs. Donovan said, "Oh, my," as her husband said, "Wouldn't put it past him. Ornery SOB."

I sat quietly for several seconds, staring at the pretty flooring.

"Drugs, you think?" Mr. Donovan asked.

"My working theory is fireworks."

"Well, dad gum," he said.

"We did hear more firecrackers than in other years. You know how it is around July. Kids set them off. Although," Mrs. Donovan paused, "I don't think we've heard them the last week or so."

I refused an offer of lemonade, which Mrs. Donovan lamented she should have offered as soon as I arrived, and drove back to town. I hadn't thought of an absence of something as important, but if the barn had stored fireworks, there certainly wouldn't be any to shoot off now.

The more I thought about it, the more certain I became that Peter Frost had earned his extra cash working with whoever used the barn. But what did he do to get himself killed?

CHAPTER FIFTEEN

I HAD DRIVEN PAST my parent's farm and had almost reached Peter Frost's when an idea occurred to me. The police were looking for – more accurately thought they had found – the killer. I was looking for a reason for Frost to be at our barn. The searches were not mutually exclusive, but they could take a person in different directions.

I drove by the Frost farm slowly. As with the Donovans' place, the barn sat behind the house. Frost's two-story house was smaller than my parents' and had only been built about forty years ago. Pretty modern for a working Iowa farm.

Though my memory of the day or two after Frost's murder was imperfect, I didn't remember seeing any police tape at his house. Granger would have let the sheriff look at anything – no warrant. And because he had not died there, the sheriff didn't do a CSI-type investigation, probably.

Would the house contain evidence of how Frost acquired the cash he'd been depositing more frequently? Could there be a computer that required no password and contained email records?

Even as I had the last thought, I discounted it. Electronic communication always left bread crumbs. If I tried to look at anything Frost had, the effort would probably lead the sheriff right to me.

It was the second of July. How early would it be dark enough to poke around?

Nine o'clock, I thought. Iowa was in the eastern part of the central time zone, so it got dark earlier than, say, Kansas. Even in farm country, cars would still be on the road at nine. I decided to wait until about eleven.

I NAPPED BETWEEN seven and ten p.m. Wednesday evening. I'm not usually a napper, but the longer this whole thing went on, the more emotionally exhausted I felt.

Mister Tibbs acted very confused. After she circled my recliner four or five times, I patted the arm of the chair. She took this as permission to join me, a special treat.

I set the alarm on my cell phone, half hoping I would oversleep and stay home. After all, I didn't know what I expected to find, and I could get arrested for breaking and entering.

Mister Tibbs and I both slept the full three hours. The alarm woke her with more of a start than it did me. From her swift glance at the door, I knew we needed a near-immediate potty trip.

When we got back upstairs, she yawned and cocked her head. It seemed she expected us to head to bed. Instead, I didn't hang up my lightweight jacket and took a bottle of water from the fridge, then put it in my pocket.

"I'll be back soon."

She lay down and rolled, exposing her belly. I stooped to scratch her.

"You won't miss me."

Her whimper said otherwise, but I stood and gently pushed a chew toy toward her.

With only a quarter moon, darkness enveloped me as I walked to my truck. I tried not to crunch the gravel much and didn't turn on my headlights until I'd driven half a block. "You're being silly. No one cares if you head out this late."

I planned to turn off my headlights when I was a quarter mile from my farm. I would pull behind the barn and leave my truck there while I hiked to Peter Frost's house.

Most farm families leave one or more doors or windows unlocked. Even if Frost did, Granger could have locked his uncle's house after his murder. Even if it was locked, I figured at least one door would have a simple doorknob lock rather than a deadbolt. I had a flat screwdriver in my jacket pocket.

I pulled into our barnyard, careful not to even pause in the spot where I often parked my pickup. Every cricket within a mile seemed to be rubbing its legs to announce me.

I drove behind the barn and turned off the engine. The silence that followed almost made my ears ring.

I nearly laughed at how softly I closed the truck door. No one could hear me.

The way to remain out of sight, so I thought, was to walk along the edge of our corn until I reached the boundary that separated our property from Frost's. His crops weren't planted as close to his house, so I'd have to walk nearly an eighth of a mile across rutted terrain that had almost knee-high grass.

I picked my way carefully. There would be no good explanation for an ambulance call for a broken ankle.

Half of me hoped I would find no way into Peter Frost's house. I touched the pair of cotton garden gloves in my jacket pocket. I didn't expect to be stopped at any point, but if I were, the garden gloves were common items for me. Latex or vinyl gloves would not be.

Not one car drove along the road. Even so, I felt relieved that the moon ducked behind a few clouds when I got near Frost's house.

As I got closer, I looked for a dog. I thought it had died before Frost, and then realized if it hadn't someone would have taken it.

I'd never been this close to his house and had not realized it was so shabby. The aged aluminum siding meant no peeling paint, but the porch that ran across most of the front of the house had unpainted boards that looked like recent replacements for rotten ones. Perhaps Granger or someone had done the work after Frost died.

Implements in various states of rust cluttered the area just behind the house – a push lawnmower, two large tubs that probably had held water for livestock at some point, and a single metal swing. Smaller items littered the back porch – an old rake, empty plastic milk cartons, and overturned bowls.

Something brushed against my leg. I jumped and pulled away. The small, clearly malnourished, gray cat wound between my legs and meowed loudly.

"Damn." My pocket had half of a dog treat, and I pulled it out. The cat smelled it and meowed more noisily. She butted my calf as I stooped, crushed half of the treat in my hand, and held it out. She nearly ate my palm.

"I'm sorry, girl. If I'd known you were here, I would've taken you home with me." She gobbled the rest of the treat and looked at me expectantly.

I climbed the three steps onto the back porch and turned a bowl over. She – I assumed a girl, since she didn't have the large head many males have – stuck her nose in it and looked up expectantly. I took the bottle of water from my pocket and poured half in the bowl.

She drank with gusto. I left her to it and put on my gloves before I touched the porch door knob. It was locked, but the door rattled gently. No deadbolt.

Before I used the flathead screwdriver to try to open it, I went to the two windows that faced the back porch. The first was locked, the second wasn't.

The windows were single-paned and, given the rotting caulk, probably let in every gust of wind. I shook my head slightly. Rusting stuff in the yard was less a sign of poverty than leaky windows.

I had no idea Peter Frost lived like this. Or maybe he had money and hadn't cared to keep his place in better shape.

Clouds moved, and the moon cast a bit of light. A glance through the porch window showed the kitchen. The chairs boasted piles of newspapers, and the counters had a mix of canisters, seed packets, and shaving supplies. Typical bachelor, I thought.

The floor was clean, and dishes were stacked neatly in the drainer. I wondered if someone, maybe Aaron Granger, had cleaned up a bit after Frost died.

The window creaked as I raised it, but no one would be near enough to hear it. Before I could raise a leg to enter, the cat leapt onto the sill and into the kitchen.

"Damn, damn, double damn!"

It scampered to the cabinet door under the sink and began to paw at it.

"I guess we know where your food is."

I climbed into the dark kitchen, shut the window, and pulled my pencil flashlight from the pocket of my jeans. I didn't need to turn it on to open the cupboard. As soon as I did, the cat darted in.

A bag of cat food tumbled onto the floor and the cat flew out and pawed it. I stooped and unfastened a clip, which let food pour onto the floor. I let her eat her fill and walked from the kitchen into the living room.

The house was a center hall colonial, though I doubted the builder had used that term. The first floor had four rooms – living room, dining room, kitchen, and office – with stairs in the center that led to an upstairs.

I started with the cluttered office. I hoped to find something that said Frost had dealings with whoever had used our barn. It was a longshot, but I had no short answers.

The wooden desk was light-colored, like old teachers' desks, and just as scarred. The drawers opened with protest, yielding a few pens and pencils, paper, bank statements, and several prior years' copies of the *Farmer's Almanac*.

At first, I decided against opening the bank statements. The cash deposits would probably be the most relevant information, and I knew about them. I closed the drawer. Then I changed my mind, reopened it, and took out the statements.

When did the deposits start? Probably there would be no way to tell changes in deposit patterns, but maybe I'd get lucky.

January through April of the current year showed Peter Frost received Social Security deposits and small monthly credits from some sort of financial firm. A 401K or something like that, I presumed. The fairly low income level partially explained the shabbiness.

He didn't seem to use an ATM card. Instead, he wrote checks to places such as the Hy-Vee grocery store, the local electric co-op, and a seed company.

Things changed in May. A two-hundred dollar cash deposit appeared on the tenth, and another on the twentieth. Then there was another one on the thirtieth.

June saw the same on the tenth, but the amount went up to four hundred dollars on the twenty-first. That was just a few days before he died.

I closed the drawer and turned off my penlight. After staring at the desktop for several seconds, I placed my elbows on the desk and rested my chin on my balled fists. If Frost had taken a part-time job, it probably would have been in the obit.

In Chicago, people might not think two hundred dollars was a lot, but in our part of Iowa it could pay one month's electric and phone bills and a satellite dish subscription. If you didn't have a lot of extra channels.

Wishful thinking did not yield copies of an extortion note in which Frost threatened to go to the sheriff if someone didn't provide bigger paydays. Or a note from the someone telling him to back off or else.

I stood to walk upstairs when headlights bounced on Frost's driveway. Acid bubbled at the base of my throat. How could anyone know I'd broken in?

Frost had a long driveway, so I figured I had a minute, maybe two if the driver dawdled before coming into the house. And they would come in. Why else drive onto the property at nearly midnight?

I stooped and made my way to the kitchen. Two car doors slammed in front of the house. Where could I hide?

The cat had stopped eating and gazed at me with drooping eyelids. Then she straightened and zoomed down a stairway I had not spotted. The narrow opening was more like a food pantry. It had been partially open, and I hadn't searched it yet.

I walked down into a musty cellar that was darker than the interior of a locked trunk. I turned on my penlight just long enough to spot a huge boiler on the far side of the cellar. As I slunk behind it, the sound of the cat pawing in a litter box reached me. That explained her quick bolt downstairs.

Few farm families used the front door unless they had company, and whoever had arrived was no exception. There was a faint jiggling of keys, and the back door opened.

I squatted and closed my eyes. Thank God I hadn't jimmied the door. I knew I'd closed the kitchen window. I hadn't wanted the cat to get back out.

Said feline raced up the steps, and a man made a startled cry. "Bear! I looked all over for you!"

Aaron Granger, I was sure of it.

A second voice, this one I thought Newt Harmon's, said, "What do you want with a barnyard cat?"

Aaron's voice was muffled, and I could almost see him putting the cat up to his face. "She was an inside cat. She got out the day… The day we came over here to search."

So much for the gruff deputy persona Granger usually had.

"I don't get why you think she'd be here," Newt said.

Gulp. I knew they weren't talking about the cat.

"I was sitting at the speed trap just off the square, and I saw her truck go by. When I got off a few minutes ago, I checked the Keyser place. No pickup parked there."

Newt's tone sounded like that of someone trying to reason with a person in distress. Which he probably was. "Listen, Aaron, she has friends in town. She could be anywhere."

Granger apparently ignored him. "I put food on the porch for you. I didn't know you'd be locked in here. No water for days."

"My dog drinks from the toilet," Newt said.

I was familiar with that option.

"Looks like she finally got into the food under the sink. She's awful thin. Must have taken her a while to get it open."

"Aaron, I'm on duty. I can't stay here long."

"I know. If she was here I didn't want to be the one to find her."

"I don't see her truck here," Newt said. "You want me to look upstairs?"

"Would you? I'll put Bear in my car."

A thump and light running brought Bear to the top of the stairs that led to the cellar.

"Bear. Come on. You're coming home with… Damn!"

Bear had run down the steps.

I'm not sure my heart ever beat that hard. If the cat came to greet me, I'd have a one-way ticket to the county jail.

Granger's heavier footfalls started down the stairs. "Kitty, kitty. Come on, Bear."

Bear stood next to the boiler, yellow eyes blinking through the dark. I made a shooing gesture. She turned and walked away.

A clicking noise led to dim light. Probably a single bulb, but more than enough to see me if Granger were to look behind the old boiler.

"What do you have? Okay, string. Is that what you came down here for?"

He had to have a lousy nose. I could smell the litter box from fifteen feet away. I'd have figured old Bear came down to use it.

Granger grunted and bent over. "I got you, girl."

Bear meowed mildly, and Granger turned off the light. He started up the stairs, seemingly carrying Bear.

Newt and Granger apparently met in the living room. Newt said, "No one up there. Listen, maybe you need a break, some time off."

"Damn it, Newt. She hated my uncle, and now she thinks." He stopped.

"Thinks what?"

"That ass-hole Hal Morris was writing a stupid book about some people who died in a car accident. He made it sound as if it was her parents and my uncle might've fixed the brakes on their car."

So he did read it when the sheriff had my pickup!

The silence was what novelists call protracted.

"Listen, Aaron, I didn't know Morris. I mean, he was a jerk, but who would believe some piece of crap book he wrote?"

"She would. That Perkins broad would. She used to work for him."

Finally, Newt said, "I gotta get back on the road. Lucky there hasn't been a radio call the last few minutes."

I was afraid Granger would stick around, but Bear had been a good diversion. As the two men left, Granger's tone was calmer as he had a friendly chat with Bear about where she would sleep.

For a full minute after I heard car engines start, I sat on the cellar floor. My heart slowed to a normal beat. I leaned against the limestone wall and wiped sweat from my forehead.

Scurrying noises reached me. I stood and brushed off the seat of my jeans. I hoped it was a mouse or ground squirrel and not a slithering snake.

Ears on alert, I crept up the cellar stairs. I sat on the top step, where I couldn't be seen through any window should Granger come back, and simply thought.

If Granger had made a copy of Hal's mangled prose, he would have something to show the county attorney. Something that might sound like a reason for Ambrose and me to be even angrier at Frost.

But for the manuscript to be used against Ambrose, Granger would have to admit he had read it while it was in the sheriff's custody. Read it, and probably not shared it with Gallagher.

And he wouldn't have shared it. Hal's ideas, even if true, couldn't be proven. Could they?

The intense fire the night of my parents' accident surely made it nearly impossible for anyone to tell if the car had been tampered with before the wreck. How would Peter Frost have known to damage a car enough to make it crash, but not right away? And was he really that determined to get my parents' farm?

I hated Peter Frost for putting Ambrose and me through two years of anger and uncertainty. And for getting his ass murdered in our barn. But I didn't think he killed my parents.

I couldn't think he did that. Years of being a journalist, even for a small paper, had taught me to evaluate information thoroughly. I could not associate Hal's book with my parents' death. At least, not now.

I stood, debating whether to leave through the kitchen window or door. I decided on the window, since I wasn't sure the door would lock behind me.

The window's creak sounded like fingernails on a school chalkboard. I grimaced as I climbed out and shut the rickety window.

I began to walk the distance from Frost's house to my barn quickly, not even being careful to duck into a row of corn. No one else would drive on these gravel roads at nearly midnight.

I was wrong.

Just as the moon came back out from behind a cloud, dust swirled on the road. Someone was driving maybe forty-five miles per hour, and when they got to my farm, they turned into the yard and parked immediately next to the house.

I lay flat. I wasn't close enough to our corn to duck into it, and anyone looking toward Frost's house would see me standing up.

My cheek rested on the damp grass for several seconds. A car door opened, and I raised my head. Two figures, dressed in dark clothes, sprinted from the car into the cornfield.

What the heck?

Corn leaves are as sharp as a knife, but no one cursed. Had they said anything, sound would have carried in the nighttime silence.

In less than thirty seconds, the two dark figures came out of the field. Each carried a large plastic tub with a lid. They must have been heavy, as the men trudged slowly to the car. A green car, I thought, though it could have been black.

Each went to a different back car door, opened it, and shoved their box onto the back seat. They literally jumped into the driver's and front passenger seats, before the car started.

I raised my head more. Neither man, I thought they were both men, would be looking in my direction. As they pulled back onto the road, I squinted at the car. It looked like an older Ford or, maybe, a Dodge. I'd never been good telling cars apart.

I couldn't see the license plate, not even to discern the state.

I stood, slowly. Whatever that cornfield might have yielded to prove Ambrose's innocence, I'd never find it.

CHAPTER SIXTEEN

I SLEPT FITFULLY and finally got out of bed at eight Thursday morning, late for me. Mister Tibbs and I went down the steps for a quick potty trip. I forgot to feed her when we got back upstairs, that is until she tripped me as I walked toward my bedroom.

I showered and dressed, thinking about what I'd found in Frost's house and wishing I had someone to talk to about it. Even though Sandi said she hadn't written the nasty piece about Ambrose's hearing, I didn't feel too friendly toward anyone at the *South County News*.

Ambrose would howl louder than Sheriff Gallagher if I told him about the bank statements. That left Stooper, maybe. Or maybe Syl. He was some hotshot analyst.

I had no more work to do at Syl's until he thought of another project, but that didn't mean I couldn't stop by. I put on jeans, but wore a light blue cotton top rather than one of the various tee shirts I usually sported.

He's a friend, I reminded myself. You aren't going to his place for a date.

Syl's shiny pick-up sat in his driveway, and I pulled in behind it. His office was on the opposite side of his house. Unless he looked out a window, he'd know I was around only if I rang the doorbell.

When he hadn't answered in thirty seconds or so, I sat on one of his porch chairs. I knew from past experience that he talked on the phone a lot. Sure enough, after another minute he opened the front door and gestured that he would be out when he was off the phone.

I stared at his lawn, trying not to pay attention to a spot that really could use some reseeding. My mind went back to our farm.

The idea of someone using the barn to store fireworks was so firmly rooted in my brain, maybe I had overlooked something. Same thing with Frost being paid to not snitch on whoever used it. That was my idea. Maybe it was stupid.

I reminded myself that the two men who carried tubs out of the cornfield had been very real. But the contents didn't have to be fireworks. It could have been cigarettes or marijuana.

I didn't think there was much profit in anything else so easily transported. Well, jewels or gold coins, of course, but I hadn't heard about any burglaries.

Nelson and his cousin sold fireworks, but I still thought them too dull-witted to have used my parents' barn without detection. Besides, lots of other people in South County could use extra income. Almost every farmer had taken a hit the last couple years because the price of corn was down.

I couldn't think of where to go with a list of suspects based on needing money. Though, the more I thought about it, there were lots of options.

Starting pay at the meat packing plant was twelve dollars an hour – not a lot, especially if you had kids. Sandi and Ryan barely got above minimum wage. Shirley probably made more than they did. I smiled. Shirley could be a good source of ideas about who was in a big financial pinch.

Syl's screen door opened, and he came onto the porch carrying two bottles of water. "You don't usually just visit."

I held out my hand for the cool drink. "True. I'm hoping you won't charge me consulting rates for a conversation."

He sat across from me and smiled wryly. "You did fertilize my tomato plants for free."

"Ah, yes." I took a sip of water. "I have a theory about what brought Peter Frost to our barn, but no way to prove it had anything to do with getting him killed."

I laid out my Frost-as-extortionist theory and mentioned the cash deposits.

Syl frowned. "Damn, I hope those bankers aren't so loose-lipped about my finances."

"I, um, think it was a combination of Frost being dead and Melissa Martin knowing Ambrose pretty well."

"Sure. Not the point, anyway. Those deposits weren't big enough to make anyone pay attention to them. Still, you can tell your brother's lawyer you heard Frost had more cash than usual."

"I can ask her if she's subpoenaing Frost's financial records. Charlotte Dickey, that's his lawyer, might ask why I know that. I can say I heard it in the diner, and the person doesn't want their name brought in."

Syl thought for a few seconds. "We aren't talking about hiding the kind of money you don't want the IRS or Drug Enforcement to know about, but Frost could've gotten more than he put in the bank."

"You mean he might have some hidden?"

"Worth looking for more."

I hadn't planned on going back to Frost's place, but what Syl said made sense. "Hmm. I'll have to think about where to look."

Syl pointed his water bottle in my direction. "I would've expected you to jump up and run out there."

I smiled briefly. "I usually schedule forays after dark. Besides... Oh, I forgot one thing."

"Only one?"

"Last night, as I left Frost's place, two men pulled onto our property."

Syl sat up straighter. "What time was that?"

"About twelve-thirty this morning."

"And what? Did they get out of their car?"

"They did." I described their run into the cornfield and retrieval of what seemed to be heavy plastic tubs."

"Damn." He stared at one of the trellises for a moment. "Car? Truck? Did you recognize it?"

"Car. American, I think, four door, not an SUV. Dark color. I thought black or dark green, but..." I stopped. Why did the idea of a green car seem important?

I looked at Syl. "You know the Donovans? They live just east of my parents' place."

He shook his head. "If I didn't see you and Stooper or grab coffee at the diner, I could go two weeks without talking to anyone in River's Edge."

"Farmers, of course. When I visited them a few days ago, Mr. Donovan said he saw a green car in our yard once, but it was gone when he went down to see who drove it. Frost was there, too, and I guess Mr. Donovan thought Frost was checking on the car, too."

"Might be a coincidence."

"You can kind of tell the place is vacant. Could've been someone driving by, who stopped to see if it was for sale." I half-shrugged. "Or maybe whoever drove into the barn from the back used that car. I've been thinking truck, but it could have been a car."

"You said it looked like boxes or something else flat had been stored in there. Did it look like a lot of them? That might take a truck."

"Good point, Mr. Insurance Analyst."

"Mr. Insurance Data System Designer."

"Seems the same to me." When Syl frowned slightly, I said, "I more or less know the difference."

"You might just pass on the information about the car and big tubs to your friendly sheriff."

I snorted.

"I'm serious. They probably have pictures of cars of varied models. Or online links, nowadays. Maybe something will look like the car you saw."

"Something to think about. I figure it's fifty-fifty he'd arrest me for being on Frost's property, which is the only way I could have seen the guys without them seeing me."

"You don't want me telling you what to do, but I wouldn't be much of a friend if I didn't tell you to stop looking into this. Guys who come at midnight to retrieve what's probably stolen goods? You don't need them looking for you."

"I'll be careful."

Syl shook his head and made to stand.

Then I remembered I hadn't told him about Hal's book. Hadn't talked about it with anyone, since I was avoiding Sandi.

"One more thing." I outlined the plot, which only an obtuse local reader would not recognize as similar to my parents' accident.

Syl was silent for several seconds. "Does it matter? It does if it's true, of course, but how would you prove it? And don't those pages seem to be a motive to murder Frost?"

"Oh, crud." My stomach roiled. I decided not to tell Syl that Granger had read those pages.

WHEN I LEFT SYL'S, I felt marginally better for having talked to someone. Especially since his point about Hal's book might be a reason to low-key talking to people about it. Marginally better, but still unsure how to prove Ambrose's innocence.

I drove to my place to get Mister Tibbs and then toward our farm. I rolled my shoulders, hoping to shake off my sense of melancholy. Not that looking at the house and barn would be a cure for melancholy.

I had no desire to make another trip to Frost's the day before the Fourth of July. I tried telling myself that if Ambrose and Sharon were having a barbeque on the Fourth, I should try to relax, too.

As a kid I'd celebrated in the park by the river all day on the Fourth. The Rotary Club had a Pancake Breakfast, and the Lions Club sponsored games.

Ambrose stopped letting me play opposite him in the water balloon toss when I deliberately broke one on his head. At that time, I hadn't appreciated that teenage boys wanted to be cool without having water dripping down the back of their shirts.

I pulled into our farm yard and looked from the house to barn. Nothing appeared any different in daylight. Maybe I'd trek into the corn to see where corn had been trampled from storing the tubs.

I pulled to the back of the barn. If someone from the sheriff's office came by or, God forbid, reporters, I didn't want to announce my presence.

Mister Tibbs jumped out of the pickup. She circled herself and looked at me as if to ask "are you sure I'm not supposed to be on a leash?"

I smiled, and she took off.

Until finding her, I'd been around tons of dogs, but none was truly mine. The closest was a German Shepherd that followed my dad from chore to chore for years.

I'd reached the front of the barn and shut my eyes. That dog's name was, appropriately, Buddy. He died about two months before my parents did. People can move on, but Buddy would have been lost without my dad. Still, I wished I'd had Buddy after Mom and Dad died.

I opened my eyes and looked at the house. It hit me that I hadn't gone in because of Ken Brownberg's advice to stay mostly off the property until the hearing about Frost's claim on the farm.

Frost was dead. Before I looked in the corn, I would go inside my parents' house.

Since turning in my key to the *South County News* when Hal fired me, I'd had only three on my ring – my apartment, the pickup, and my parents' home. I had planned to enter in triumph, with Ambrose of course, when Frost's lawsuit was tossed out.

Who needed a judge's decision? I felt almost lightheaded as I walked up the steps.

As soon as I went in, I knew something wasn't right. My ears went on high alert, but I heard no one.

The smells. Cooking smells. Not baking, maybe hotdogs.

I stood in the door and looked at the living room and into the kitchen. Ambrose and I had moved out all the furniture when Frost filed his breach-of-contract suit. Sitting in the corner on the right, near the hall leading to the bedrooms, was a chaise lounge chair.

I wasn't afraid. Or so I told myself. No one would be in the house, the place had had too much law enforcement around recently.

I let my eyes slowly rove the room. No dust balls in the corners. There should have been. No spider webs graced the corners of the ceiling.

Mister Tibbs pawed at the screen door and I opened it so she could join me.

She padded behind me as I walked into the kitchen. A camping burner with a can of Sterno fuel sat in the sink.

Someone is living here.

On the far end of the Formica counter was an open coffee can. It was full of cigarette butts. My mother would have had a fit to think of someone smoking in her house.

I ignored the door to the cellar where my mother had stored preserves, and walked through the living room and into the largest bedroom. Two blankets sat under the window, neatly folded. Mister Tibbs bounded onto them and sat, wagging her tail.

From the hall, a voice said, "Don't turn around."

I stood still. From the window I could see my pickup and part of the barn. No one would know if this man shot me and ran.

I felt certain it was a man. He seemed to be trying to disguise his voice by speaking so low his voice sounded like a growl.

He cleared his throat. "That closet on your right. Go sideways. Don't turn around! Don't even think about it."

I couldn't think about much. My heart was beating so hard and fast I almost felt dizzy. In my peripheral vision, I saw Mister Tibbs cock her head. She was looking at the man.

What if he hurt her? My surge of anger was so strong I almost wheeled to face him, but I stopped myself just in time.

Think, think. Even if the man left now, I knew nothing to identify him. I shut my eyes, and a cigarette popped into my brain. He smelled like cigarettes.

After the few steps to the door, I said, "Now what?"

The person backed up a step or two. "Open the door, and get in there. Don't look back! Pull the door shut when you're in."

"Don't hurt my dog."

"You do what I say, and I won't."

I opened the closet door with my right hand, sidled into the small space, and pulled the door shut. As it clicked shut, Mister Tibbs barked several times.

"Quiet, girl."

"Shut up! Both of you."

I stayed quiet. I heard Mister Tibbs' nails on the hardwood floor. She must have jumped off the blankets.

"You stay in there 'til I tell you to come out."

The man left the room, and I heard him in the kitchen. He made no effort to be quiet. When I heard metal clank on metal, it occurred to me that he was packing up his supplies.

Mister Tibbs sniffed near the base of the closet.

I whispered, "It'll be okay, girl."

Even if the man removed all his things, there had to be fingerprints around the house. I hoped I'd be alive when the sheriff found them.

The sheriff! I slid my phone out of the pocket of my jeans. Whoever this was, he had the brains of a newborn calf. Leaving me with a phone marked him as a total amateur.

But amateur what? Fireworks seller? Burglar? I shivered. Murderer?

I ran my fingers over the phone until I was certain which buttons were for 9-1-1. Then I covered the receiver with my thumb so no one could hear the sheriff's dispatcher talk to me.

"Nine-one-one. What's your emergency?"

I said nothing. From having accidentally butt-dialed the dispatchers a couple of times, I knew they had to call back if you disconnected.

"Sir, ma'am? Can I help you?"

The voice was that of a woman. I tried to picture her face. She'd been hired only last year. I pictured someone in her mid-forties with a severe bun and very starched uniform collar.

"Please say something."

I blew into the phone.

"Do you need assistance? What is your emergency?"

If only I were a Star Trek telepath. I realized she'd have to be, too, and almost giggled.

I pressed the end button.

Oh, crud! I needed to mute the ringer! The light of the phone let me start the process. Just before I finished, the phone gave half a ring.

Running footsteps came from the kitchen.

"You bitch! You have a phone!" He stopped outside the closet.

"Yes, but I didn't answer it."

Mister Tibbs had apparently left the bedroom while I dialed. She now followed him into the room. She didn't bark. He must have made friends with her. Would it be harder to kill a dog you petted?

He had forgotten to lower his voice, but did it now. "I'm standing behind this door. I'm going to open it an inch. You keep your eyes shut and slide that phone out on the floor."

I pushed the phone's Off button, so he couldn't see my last call. "Okay. Whatever you say."

The door creaked as he opened it. I needed to put oil on the hinges. *Who gives a damn about hinges?!*

I stooped and pushed the phone out. I leaned over, hoping to see the guy's shoes, but all I saw was thick tread. They must be boots. So, probably not an accountant or doctor.

Mister Tibbs gave a small yip.

"Hush, dog."

"Her name is Mister Tibbs."

He pushed the door shut and walked out of the room.

I sat on the closet floor. Maybe knowing a dog's name would keep someone from killing it.

My phone let someone see my number if I called them. My big hope was that because the nine-one-one call ended, someone at the sheriff's office would come to the farm.

First they'd probably go to my apartment. Then they might call the diner. They had to call until they found who made the emergency call, right?

The man walked back into the room. "Stay in the goddamned closet." He left.

The front door slammed. It didn't make sense to come out so quickly. He might be back.

Within thirty seconds or so, he came up the back steps again. Slowly. It sounded as if he pulled something heavy behind him.

What would he be pulling? If he was clearing out of the house, he wouldn't be bringing more in.

I hadn't seen a car. Where had the guy been? The door that led from the kitchen to the cellar popped into my brain.

He came back into the room, still tugging something behind him. Something coarse.

Nuts! Just to the right of the outside steps was that pile of flagstones. *Damn, he wants to block the closet so I can't get out!*

I got on my knees and looked out the crack at the bottom of the door. Sure enough, I could just barely see the bottom edge of one of the heavy stones. They probably weighed twenty-five pounds or more. It had to make a long scratch on the floor.

"If those are my dad's stones, you're paying to refinish the floor." *What a stupid thing to say.*

"Shut up, bitch. Stay in there!"

Even if he continued to stack all the stones, I could probably get out. It'd be well more than one-hundred pounds, but I was tough.

When the man left the room, I blindly touched the closet walls to gauge its exact size. The closet was too long for me to brace my feet on the back wall to push, but I had on my boots. A lot more traction than sandals.

He made four more trips, each time breathing hard. Mister Tibbs wasn't with him for the fifth. Maybe she went outside. That would be good.

I didn't notice the cigarette smell as much. Could he have taken off a jacket? Or maybe I was getting used to the odor.

In the low voice, he said, "Listen. You stay in the damn closet. I got some stuff to do, then I'm going. You come out, I'll strangle your dog."

"I'm not coming out."

Strangle! If he'd been nice to Mister Tibbs, she'd go right to him. I'd have to stay in the closet until I hadn't heard him for a good while.

How would I know when he left? I hadn't heard a car. Duh. If it had been parked well down the road, I wouldn't have seen it. One thing for sure, it wasn't in the barn.

I could hear him moving around the house, but not quickly. What could he be doing? With a sinking feeling, I realized he was probably wiping everything, getting rid of fingerprints.

The side door banged a few times as he went in and out. Finally, five minutes had gone by since I thought I'd heard him in the house. How long should I wait?

I still hadn't heard a car start.

And where the hell is the sheriff?

After two or three minutes more, I called, "Mister Tibbs!"

No bark responded, so I tried again. Still nothing.

"Oh my God! He took Mister Tibbs!!"

I leaned my back against the door, planted my feet firmly, and pushed. Nothing.

"You idiot, turn the handle."

I jiggled the knob. There was no lock, but the stones kept the door firmly shut. Sweat ran down the side of my right cheek.

I'd have to keep the door knob twisted to keep the latch knob out of the switch plate in the wall. That meant standing.

Leverage when I stood was much less than when I sat, but I kept pushing with my shoulder and calling for Mister Tibbs. The door barely opened an inch. It was enough so I could let go of the knob while I continued to push.

Five minutes later, even my back was sweaty. Tears tickled my cheeks. I rested by sitting on the floor, putting my head on my knees, and massaging my neck.

As I stood, the sound of a car on gravel came into the yard. I yelled, "I'm in here! In the closet!"

No car door seemed to open. "Damn, if they have the air conditioning on, they won't hear me!"

The car seemed to back up. Rage and fear alternated, and I screamed. Surely they'd hear that.

The car kept backing up. Then it stopped, and a door opened.

Now I really was crying. They heard me!

But, they hadn't. They'd heard Mister Tibbs. She was coming closer, barking nonstop.

A man's voice said, "Whoa, girl. Whoa."

Mister Tibbs ran up the side steps and kept barking.

"Okay, I'm coming," the man said. Not the same man who had locked me in the closet.

I rubbed my hand across my cheeks to wipe tears. When the man seemed to be near the steps, I yelled, "In here! I'm in the closet!"

"Melanie?" He jiggled the house door, but my keeper had apparently locked it.

"Newt? Deputy Harmon?"

"Yeah. You're stuck? What's going on?"

"Just come in and get me out."

"Is there a key out here?"

Oh, crud. Now I know how someone got in. "If it's not taped under a bottom step, use a crowbar, or break a window." My voice was getting hoarse from yelling.

The sound of my voice had quieted Mister Tibbs. I remembered she'd seen Newt several times. He'd even petted her one day down by the river.

Newt came back up the steps. "I'm gonna break one of the panes on the door."

Glass tinkled and he must have reached in, because I could hear him fumbling with the door handle lock. The door had a deadbolt, but whoever had been using the house must not have taken the time to lock it from the outside.

That was lucky. If the deadbolt had been locked from the outside, Newt would have to break down the door. I swore I'd never hide a key again.

The door opened. Mister Tibbs ran in and came to my room.

"Hey, dog. Come back here."

"I'm in here, Newt. In the closet."

He walked into the room and stopped. "Somebody put you in there?"

"Gee, you think?" I told myself not to be rude to a rescuer.

"I'll get you out." His radio crackled. "I need somebody else at the Perkins' place. Mel must have surprised a burglar or something."

CHAPTER SEVENTEEN

AS NEWT HARMON had observed, I clearly hadn't locked myself in a closet with about 150 pounds of flagstones outside it. No one doubted what happened.

However, I had no description of my captor, and unless the sheriff's deputies had missed a spot, there were no fingerprints. Once again, there was no proof to help find the bad guy.

Within an hour of being found, I was in Sheriff Gallagher's office with Mister Tibbs asleep at my feet. I had refused to go into the building without her. I sat at his small conference table, my back to the hallway door, with Gallagher and Newt Harmon across from me.

"Cigarette smell and sort of deep, gravelly voice. Nothing else at all?"

"Mister Tibbs saw him. I didn't."

Gallagher just stared at me. "She isn't a cooperative witness."

I shut my eyes briefly, took a deep breath, and let it out. "I'm sorry I was snarky."

"I'd be upset, too. Good thing you hung up on nine-one-one."

"I didn't have a lot of choice. I'm glad you guys followed through." I nodded at Newt. "Especially you."

He nodded, with a worried expression that had not left him since he'd found me.

"And you heard no car," Gallagher said.

I didn't remind him we'd already discussed this. "My truck was in the barn. My keys were still on a kitchen counter when Newt found me."

Gallagher nodded. "So, if they'd wanted your truck, they could have taken it. Probably had a car nearby."

"If it was me," Newt said, "I'd have taken your keys."

I thought about that. "I guess the guy didn't think I'd be getting out anytime soon."

Gallagher made a note on his yellow pad. "Probably didn't want to be seen driving your pickup, so he didn't want to take it."

Newt and I both said, "Good point."

I figured Newt was sucking up. I wasn't. I hadn't considered that, but it made sense. If someone did not want to be seen in my truck, did it make it more or less likely that the person was from South County?

"Wish you'd told us earlier today about the boxes in the field," Gallagher said.

"Me, too, now. I couldn't think of how to do it." I'd just told them I was in Frost's yard at midnight. I didn't mention I'd been in the house.

"Humph. I can see why. What in the hell were you looking for?"

"Anything that would show Ambrose didn't kill Peter Frost."

"Not sure that's the best place to look." Gallagher glanced at his notes. "Let's go over one more time what you saw in your house."

"You wrote it down. I think the guy must have stayed there some, guarding the goods in the barn."

"Goods that, if they were there, are long gone."

"Maybe they took the last boxes last night and then came back to get the stuff from the house today."

"Seems odd," Newt said. "They must've been pretty sure you and Ambrose wouldn't go in the house."

"Convenient," came Granger's voice from the door.

Gallagher looked at his deputy and frowned. "Granger."

I turned to face him, noting Granger's rigid posture and arms folded across his chest. "So they must be local. Lots of people knew I drove out there once or twice a week, but because of the lawsuit, I didn't go in the house."

"Aaron, you can't be in here."

Granger's face was a mix of anger and something else. "Did you see a cat when you were trespassing last night?"

I feigned surprise. "Funny you ask. I thought I heard one, but I couldn't find it."

"You aren't a very good investigator," he said.

"Granger, out." Gallagher's tone was firm.

Granger turned and left. His footsteps in the hall sounded like marching boots.

Newt cleared his throat. "Uh, sheriff. Granger and I were, uh, at his uncle's place last night."

Gallagher's face began to redden, and he turned slightly to face Newt. "Will I find that on our blotter?"

"No sir."

"Put it there. Why the hell were you out there?"

Deputy Harmon, who was in full deputy mode now, explained about Granger seeing my car in town at about eleven-thirty and then not seeing it at Mrs. Keyser's.

Gallagher sounded as if he was holding back a good holler. "And you saw what at Frost's place?"

"Just the cat. Must've gotten locked in the house. Really thin. Granger took it."

"Too bad cats don't talk either." Gallagher turned to me. "You see those two?"

I shook my head. "I was pulling out when I saw headlights in the distance. I turned toward the Donovans' place and took the long way back into town."

Gallagher started to say something, but I interrupted. "And I parked behind the barn. No one could see my car from the road, Frost's or the Donovans' place. That's how they, the murderer, got into the barn without being seen."

"They," he muttered. In a normal tone, he said, "Harmon, get that on the blotter, and when Ms. Perkins is gone, you tell Granger I want to see him."

Newt left, and Gallagher stared at me for a good two or three seconds. A long time when a person feels like they're on the hot seat.

"Melanie, this is odd. But you and I know it doesn't change much. Ambrose was holding that knife."

I swallowed. "But it should raise some questions."

"I will go so far as to say it might. It could also be a homeless guy figured where the hell you kept the spare key and was staying out of the rain."

"A homeless person wouldn't lock me in the closet."

He shrugged. "Homeless or not, could have been someone trying to stay off anybody's radar. Not a good person to be alone in a house with."

I nodded. "If I'd had a clue anyone was in there, I would have called you."

Gallagher snorted. "Go over again when you were last in the house."

I did, and he tapped a pencil eraser on the table. "Can't have been anyone in there too long. Would've been seen."

Mister Tibbs seemed to have heard the pencil taps, because she stirred and looked up at me.

"In a few minutes," I told her.

"Your dog hadn't come running up the road, you'd have been in that closet 'til you could get yourself out or Sandi or somebody raised an alarm."

"Running down the road?"

"Didn't Newt tell you? She came running from toward the Donovans'."

I whispered, "He took her with him."

"Huh, maybe. Didn't want her barking at the house, probably."

I looked down at Mister Tibbs and back at the sheriff. "I think he petted her. At least she got quieter around him after a minute or two. Can you get prints from a dog's fur?"

"Don't think so, but maybe the collar. I'll have to send it to the state police for something like that. Our equipment's not very refined."

Before either one of us spoke again, Sophie knocked on the door jamb. "Sheriff? Mr. Seaton's here to see about Melan...Ms. Perkins."

"Melanie," I said, without looking at her.

"Tell him she'll be out in a minute." He looked at me. "You call him?"

I started to say it was none of his business, but said only, "No, but since I rode here in Newt's car and we're a block from the diner, everyone I know could probably tell you I'm here."

He shook his head. "Anything else? About this morning or any late-night visits. To anywhere."

I crossed my fingers, which were under the table. "No, and if I knew something I'd tell you."

He stood. "Don't go anywhere unaccompanied for a while. Better yet, visit Ambrose for a few days."

I stood, as did Mister Tibbs. But I didn't yawn when she did. "He and Sharon are having a Fourth of July barbeque at their place. He didn't invite me."

Gallagher laughed. "Imagine that."

THE COLLARLESS MISTER TIBBS and I were in Syl's living room later Thursday, at the grouping of chairs in front of his fireplace. Mister Tibbs had been given enough to drink at the sheriff's office that she had watered several plants on the way into Syl's house.

While Syl put ice in glasses in the kitchen, I looked around the room. He had added a two-seat sofa in deep brown and an area rug near the fireplace.

He came back in, handed me a glass of ice water, and raised his own in a mock toast before sitting opposite me.

"Thanks again for coming to the sheriff's."

"When Shirley calls, I listen. If Sandi or Stooper can't take you to get your truck, I'll do it."

I leaned my head against the back of the Queen Anne chair for a second and sighed. "It was my own house. I'd never have thought anyone would be in there."

He shook his head, more serious now. "You're going to have to be careful even when it seems safe."

I sat up straighter. "It shows someone was using the property. That has to count for a lot."

"Did you call Ambrose?"

"Oh, crud."

He laughed out loud. "Have you noticed I've reminded you to do that on at least three prior occasions?"

I started to reach in my pocket and frowned.

"Sheriff have your phone?"

"I wish. The guy who locked me in the closet."

Mister Tibbs snored loudly, and Syl said, "Damn it all, Melanie." He reached in a pocket, pulled out his mobile phone, and stood to hand it to me.

"Thanks. This ought to be fun."

His wry grin was back. "Should I wait in another room?"

I pushed Ambrose's number. "I'm sure you've heard people get chewed out before."

As the phone rang, Syl picked up a manila folder from the end table next to his chair and opened it. I was glad he at least feigned working.

Ambrose had, of course, already heard. "And how come Sharon had to get a call from Gallagher instead of me getting one from you?"

"I wonder why he called Sharon?" I mused.

"Because he wanted the other owner of the farm to know someone broke in, and he thinks I'm a damn murderer. That's not the point!"

"The guy who locked me in the closet took my phone." Silence.

"The battery was low, so he couldn't call you either." I had tried to inject humor, but failed.

"Mel, something is really wrong at the farm. You can't be going back out there."

"I know. I'll just drive by without stopping."

"Ask the Donovans to keep an eye on the place."

I didn't sigh, but it was hard not to. "I don't know where to go from here."

"I'm talking to Ms. Dickey on the fifth. Let her handle it!"

Someone pounded on Syl's front door, and he rose to answer it.

Ambrose spoke loudly. "What was that?"

"Relax. Just somebody's at Syl's front door."

"Oh, I didn't look at the name on the phone. I'm glad you're with someone."

"I left my truck at the farm. I'll get it later today. With Sandi or somebody."

Stooper's voice came from the front hall. "What the hell, Syl?"

"Oh, I'd better go."

"I want you to call me every morning from now on."

To get off the phone quickly, I agreed.

Syl must have indicated Stooper could come into the living room, because he walked across the room and stood directly in front of my chair.

"I have to hear from Andy?"

Mister Tibbs stood up, leaning her front paws on Stooper's jeans. He patted her without looking down.

"I'm sorry, Stooper, I just left the sheriff's place." Stooper glowered, so I added, "And I don't have my phone. The guy took it."

"Shirley called me," Syl said, in his maddeningly dry manner. He sat across from me and nodded at Stooper. "Have a seat."

After hesitating for a second, Stooper sat in a chair next to Syl's.

I looked from one to the other. "I feel as if I'm on trial."

"You could end up there," Syl said. He turned to Stooper. "Andy? At the hardware store?"

"He thinks you and Mel have a thing going on."

I bent over my lap, eyes looking at the floor.

"Did he say if it was any good?" Syl asked.

I looked up, chin on my knees. Stooper laughed, showing the missing teeth on the upper right side of his mouth. "Mel's put him straight a couple of times. I think you need to do it," Stooper added.

My face felt beet red.

"I don't think I will," Syl said, easily.

TO GET AWAY from the comedy duo of Stooper and Syl and to wonder a bit if I'd like to get to know Syl better, I asked Stooper to take Mister Tibbs and me to get the pickup.

We'd done that, with me answering Stooper's ten questions. And I used to think he was quiet.

Only after he'd elicited my promise not to go to the farm alone did Stooper let me out of his car, so I could drive my pickup back to my apartment.

Now, I lay on my couch, staring at the ceiling. I'd heard Gallagher tell Newt Harmon to call my phone and Newt's response that it went directly to voice mail. Whoever took it had turned it off. So, no point trying to call my mobile.

I closed my eyes and imagined the guy's voice – the only thing I could conjure up. Meaning I had nothing. I'd told the sheriff the guy sounded white rather than Hispanic or black, but really, anyone could sound any way these days.

The voice had sounded as if it had come from a bit above my head, but that could mean five-ten or six-feet-two. There had been no chance to glimpse clothing or hair color.

I glanced at Mister Tibbs, who was on the floor. "Wish you could talk."

She thumped her tail once, but didn't open her eyes.

"How far did you have to run back?" I leaned a hand down and ruffled the top of her head. She opened one eye and closed it again.

"You're such a good girl. And you're so tired. Must've been quite a run."

Since I had no phone to use to tell time, I glanced at the clock. Two in the afternoon.

Rapid footfalls tramped up the steps on the side of the house, and someone rapped on my door. "Mel? Are you in there?"

"Just a sec, Sandi."

Mister Tibbs didn't even get up. I walked to the door and opened it.

She stared at me, mouth half open, part of her red hair hanging out of her scrunchie. "You're all right. Why didn't you call?"

I stood aside to let her in. "Shirley called Syl. He picked me up at the sheriff's."

"Not for a ride. I mean, of course I would have. I meant," she sort of stuttered, "I mean, I'm glad you're okay."

"I am, just kind of out of sorts."

I gestured she should sit on the couch or the recliner. She sat on the couch, and I sat across from her.

Sandi sighed. "Look, I told you I'm sorry. I didn't write it."

"I'm not mad at you, personally, I just don't feel like giving a story to the paper."

"I don't blame you." She leaned back into the couch. "Ryan's mother's cousin probably told us everything. I wanted to be sure you're in one piece."

I raised an eyebrow, and she had the decency to roll her eyes.

"Of course I'm happy to take anything for a story, but I'm here as your friend."

I felt my shoulders, which I hadn't realized were stiff, relax. "I believe you. But I can only tell you what I told Gallagher. A guy surprised me in the house, and I saw nothing, I mean zip, about what he looked like."

She frowned. "He was behind you?"

"Yep, and he said if I turned around he'd hurt Mister Tibbs."

From Sandi's raised eyebrows as she bent to pet the gently snoring dog, I knew Ryan had not heard about this threat from his mother's cousin.

She sat back up. "I wouldn't have tried to sneak a peek, either."

For the first time since she'd arrived, I smiled at her. "I need to get a new phone at the gas station, and then I want to find my phone. You have any ideas?"

"Can't imagine the guy would be carrying it around."

"Yeah, sheriff had Newt try it. Went to voice mail."

She looked at the ceiling for a second, her thinking position. "If it had been me, I would have tossed it out the window of my car."

"Agreed. Probably in another state."

"Get out your county map," she ordered.

I raised my eyebrows at her, but walked to the kitchen and took it from a drawer. Together we spread it on the coffee table in front of the couch.

I pointed. "Our place."

She pointed. "Frost's, and Donovans'."

Her finger trailed County Road 270 past the Donovan's for half a mile until it came to a T intersection at Tulip Avenue. "Turn right and this goes over to Highway 218."

"Sure, and from there down to Missouri or up to Iowa City. But if the phone's off, no way to track the guy."

She tilted her head. "I'd get rid of it just before I got on 218."

I looked at her. "I'd do it a mile or so past the Donovans'. At the T in the road."

She grinned. "We'll start there."

WE FIRST WENT TO the gas station and bought what the TV crime shows call a burner phone. I didn't have my number transferred to it. I had no illusion that I'd find mine, but after the Fourth of July celebrations tomorrow, I'd go to my usual provider and get a better one than the flip phone I'd bought for $9.99.

Sandi drove, and we were at the Donovans' farmhouse about three o'clock.

I looked right and left as I walked up the steps to their door. I told myself that whoever locked me in the closet was far away by now. Still, I felt mildly nervous as I knocked.

Mrs. Donovan answered, wearing a pretty shirtwaist and a look of concern. "Goodness, Melanie, come in."

"I can't stay, Sandi's in the car, and we want to look for something."

She literally shook a finger at me. "Sheriff called himself. I'm supposed to call if you come here investigating."

Mr. Donovan appeared behind her. "Now, hon, she's only investigating if she asks crime-type questions." He smiled. "Sorry to say, we were in the back of the property and didn't see anyone."

Mrs. Donovan nodded. "And like we told the sheriff, we only have cameras by the front and back door and in an area in front of the barn."

I smiled. "Good to know. I had to ask or come by."

She smiled, and he sort of snorted before he spoke. "We'll keep a better eye on your place. Not sure it'll help much, since we're in the fields a lot."

I refused two lemonades "for the road," as Mrs. Donovan put it, and headed for my truck.

Sandi grimaced when I told her we had no more to go on, but her only comment was, "Next time take the lemonade."

"Not my first priority. So, down to the T?"

Sandi loosened the cap on her bottle of water and took a swig. "We can each take one side of the road."

It was hot, and the sun was unremittingly bright. The Iowa Hawkeye hat I wore made me even hotter, since it kept in heat from my head. But I knew if I took it off, my nose would be red in ten minutes.

Sandi, pale redhead that she is, had on long sleeves and a calf-length skirt, plus a broad-brimmed straw hat. We both lathered with bug spray that had sunscreen. You never know what kinds of flying creatures will follow you around in southeastern Iowa.

We are both methodical researchers and writers, so we applied the same skills to our search. Since cornfields were on all sides, it was a slow hunt.

If it had been grass or dirt, we could have scanned quickly or at least walked slowly and looked all around. With the corn stalks, we had to stoop and peer down each row.

"It can't have been thrown too far," Sandi called from the other side of the narrow road, "the phone would have hit a stalk."

"Agreed." I shone my flashlight down a row and then moved to the next one. A couple weeks earlier, light would have made it to the ground. Now the corn was too tall.

The words from an old musical came to me. "Corn is as high as an elephant's eye..." I hummed for several seconds.

We continued walking Tulip Avenue, just east of where it intersected with 270. We would go west eventually, but everything told me my jailer would head to the highway.

To go west would wend back toward town. I thought the person would be noticed more if he went closer to town.

I stood from my crouched position. All of my thinking was based on the culprit having a car or truck. Farmers walk their fields or kids play near a pond, but no one walks along farm roads. The roads are narrow, and it can be hard to get out of the way of a tractor or hog truck.

Still, my captor could have been on foot. I wondered if the sheriff had instructed deputies to search the cornfield near my house?

"Melanie?"

I jumped. Sandi was only a few feet from me. "What?"

"I called you twice. What were you thinking?"

I took off my hat and wiped my forehead with my small towel. "If the person was on foot, where do you think they'd head?"

She shrugged. "Anybody's barn or chicken coop."

We grinned. "Not chicken coop," I said.

"Too stinky," she agreed.

I gestured around us. "They'd have to walk a couple rows into the corn if they went along the road."

"But you heard the person go in and out of the house. Didn't you think the guy was loading a car or something?"

I knocked myself lightly on the side of the head. "Yeah. Oh. Unless they were carrying things back into the field."

Sandi shook her head. "You think they drove Mister Tibbs away with them, remember?"

I sighed. "I'm glad you're thinking clearly."

She pushed sunglasses down her nose, so I could see her eyes. "I haven't been locked in a closet today."

I grinned and tried to hide my shudder by speaking lightly. "The day's young."

Sandi glanced up. "More or less. You want to drive toward the highway?"

I shook my head. "It would make sense to throw it in a corn or soybean field. Won't be found. By fall it'll be harvested or ground into the dirt."

Sandi turned toward her car. "Ugh. Come on. I didn't eat lunch. Diner?"

"How about the barbeque place? Fewer people."

JUANITA SPARKS, WHOM WE all call Momma Sparks, for some reason, was happy to see us on a warm Thursday afternoon. "When it's hot like this, everyone wants ice cream. No barbeque."

She is originally from somewhere in Eastern Europe and once told me her given name is "too complicated," so she picked Juanita. Her English seems good, and I think her stilted sentence structure and occasional malapropisms are for effect.

"So, Miss Melanie, you in trouble again. I am not liking that."

Sandi glanced at me. "It's more her brother Ambrose in trouble. Melanie's helping him."

"Ambrose not locked in closet, is he?"

If it had been someone else, I might have been irritated, but it's hard not to get a kick out of Juanita. "He's at his farm in Dubuque. Pretty soon everyone will know he didn't kill Peter Frost."

Before Juanita could say anything more, Sandi asked, "So, what's the special today?"

Juanita took a pencil and small notepad from the pocket of her wide, white apron. "You know Mr. Harris?"

"Sam?" I asked.

"Yes. Him. He bring me basket of green peppers, tomatoes, and squash. I make vegetarian barbeque. Very special price."

Sandi was still scanning the menu. "People order that a lot?"

"Why you think it's half price?"

I inhaled some of the water I'd been about to drink and picked up a paper napkin to blow my nose.

Sandi grinned at me. "I'll have some. Bring Mel your usual pork, not too spicy. My treat."

"So," Juanita asked, "you want with fries and drink, maybe pie?"

I mopped my eyes. "Just barbeque on a bun. A little coleslaw on the side."

Sandi and I didn't look each other in the eye until Juanita was back in her kitchen. Then Sandi put a napkin over her mouth, so she didn't laugh out loud.

I mopped water from the front of my shirt. "I needed that laugh."

"You did," she agreed.

My eyes roamed Juanita's small restaurant. The eight tables have red and white checkered table cloths with heavy white paper that can be removed when it gets stained. Which is after most meals, given how juicy her barbeque is.

I used to wonder how she made a living, but I've heard she caters, too. In fact, her barbeque is so popular if you want it during high school graduation weekend, you have to order by February.

"So, Mel, where are we?"

I sighed. "You know I'm no quitter, but I may give it a rest until after the Fourth. Ambrose said he and Sharon are chilling until he talks to his lawyer on the fifth."

"Closet got to you?"

I shook my head. "That the bastard almost made off with Mister Tibbs."

"Ah." She took a drink of her ice water, without inhaling any. "You still think someone had fireworks in the barn, right?"

"Yes, but I'm no closer to proving it."

She nodded, slowly. "Maybe we can ask around before the city fireworks tomorrow night."

"I already know Nelson McDonald and his cousin sell them. Somehow, I don't see them as smart enough to bring in so much product that they need a place to store it."

Sandi was thoughtful. "Nelson was smart enough to beat a fencing rap a couple of times."

"I know it's stupid, but I like that he says he doesn't think Ambrose did it."

"Where is the reporter I worked with? Maybe it's because he knows who did kill Frost."

CHAPTER EIGHTEEN

SANDI MIGHT HAVE A POINT. Maybe I was too quick to disregard Nelson as the murderer.

I decided to follow Nelson and his cousin on the Fourth. I looked at the clock. It was just past midnight Friday morning. That meant it was already Independence Day.

But follow them where, to see if they met people in the hardware store lot or somewhere else? I already knew what they sold. If I made a list of their buyers, all I'd be doing was getting other people in trouble for buying illegal fireworks.

Mister Tibbs snored from the foot of my bed. I'd never let her sleep on the bed, only on the blanket beside it. Even now, I had a towel by my feet and wouldn't let her sleep by my head. Not that she hadn't tried.

I've never been that attached to a pet. Probably because we farm kids had our 4-H cows or goats and knew where they'd end up. And barn cats. They were a nuisance.

But Mister Tibbs felt like my child. *That's silly.*

Okay, it was silly, but it was true. I didn't want to lose her. Maybe I should do as Ambrose said and mind my own business.

But that would mean County Attorney Smith would keep after Ambrose, at least for a while. To be sure my brother had the best defense, I'd sign a note saying an attorney could have the farm. Assuming we would get clear title again.

So, I'd have Mister Tibbs, but I'd lose the farm. I wanted both.

Fourth of July or not, I'd have to find a way.

THE SOFTBALL FIELD ALMOST sparkled in the Fourth of July sun. The white bases and home plate must have been washed, and the bleachers on each side of the batter's cage had been repainted. Red, white, and blue, of course.

Fifty yards or so beyond the ball field, the Des Moines River looked more blueish-green than brown. We needed a good rain to stir up the mud.

Mister Tibbs was on her leash, but she wouldn't wander even if I unhooked her. She's rarely in places with so many people and didn't seem to want to mingle.

Sandi and I were not meeting until the fireworks tonight. By that time, the softball game would be over, and Mister Tibbs would be by herself in the apartment. Part of me felt guilty about that, but she'd hate the noise near the river after dark.

We were en route to the bleachers when a woman called my name. Kate and Bill Henning were in my graduating class. I thought they lived in Cedar Rapids now.

I walked toward them. "Wow, Kate. You guys are pregnant."

"She is," Bill said.

I kissed Kate on the cheek and pulled back. "You always were a smart ass, Bill."

"Actually, we go by William and Kate now."

Kate rolled her eyes. "And if it's a boy, he wants to name him George."

"And a girl?" I teased.

Bill grinned. "Charlotte, of course. Only the best for our kid."

We were silent for a couple seconds.

Then Kate said, "I'm sorry about Ambrose."

Bill sobered. "I don't believe it."

"Thanks. Where are you guys now?"

They took my cue and stayed away from the topic. Instead, they talked about buying a house in "the cutest town ever," which is what they deemed Mount Vernon, Iowa.

Bill had an engineering degree from Iowa State, and Kate had graduated from Iowa in economics. They both worked in Iowa City, not far from Mount Vernon.

"So," I asked, "do you have one of those blankets with a Cyclone on one side and a Hawkeye on the other?"

"Got two for wedding presents," Kate said.

"All the baby clothes will be Cyclone," Bill said.

Kate threw a handful of popcorn at him.

They walked away to meet Kate's parents by the Snack Shack, and Mister Tibbs and I wandered to the river. There was little wind, and the water ran quietly. We stood in the shade near the edge of the bank.

On another day, I would have let Mister Tibbs off her leash, but today the park behind us was too crowded. Instead, she pulled me toward every tree.

A couple of high school-age boys were trying to launch a kayak from the boat ramp. I thought one looked like the big brother to Rachel, who had petted the black cat in front of Patel's store.

Both boys fell in the water twice. From the giggles a few yards from the boat ramp, it was clear they were entertaining the group of girls on a nearby picnic table.

All of them pretended to ignore each other when one of the volunteer sheriff deputies walked over. I couldn't hear the conversation, but it was obviously a gentle warning not to horse around with a boat, even in shallow water.

One boy quickly launched the first kayak, and the second pulled one into the water and followed the first.

Within half a minute, they were racing each other to the opposite shore.

"Come on, Mister Tibbs. Let's find a bench."

She wagged her short tail and led the way to one close to the small hotel, which faced the river. Several older people sat on wide, white rockers on the hotel porch. I returned a wave, though I didn't know who the man was. Probably a friend of my parents.

To avoid conversation, Mister Tibbs and I walked down river and picked a bench near the fire station. She was too short to jump onto the bench, so I lifted her to sit next to me.

For several minutes, her little head moved slowly from side to side, watching the water flow. When she gave a quick start, I followed her gaze. A tree branch was floating by.

Mister Tibbs looked at me.

"Nope. If you even tried to swim out there, you'd end up in the Mississippi." With a stab of pain, I thought of an old friend who had done just that.

I stood. "Come on. Let's see when the ball game starts."

We stayed by the river as we walked. I looked forward to cheering at the game, but not to having a lot of one-on-one conversations. Everyone would ask about Ambrose.

The day was getting close to the promised eighty-five degrees, so Mister Tibbs and I walked toward the Snack Shack. I bought a Dr. Pepper for me and a bottle of water for Mister Tibbs.

Shirley gave me a free cup. "I'm supposed to charge, Shug, but I hear your Mister Tibbs saved your bacon yesterday."

I nodded. "I'll come by tomorrow and tell you all about it."

By the time I got to the diner, the *South County News* would have published a story, so I wouldn't have to talk a lot.

As I began to walk to the bleachers, a familiar voice said, "Mel?"

I turned halfway, but didn't stop. "Ryan."

He reached me, and we walked side by side. "Look, I had to write it that way."

"Don't talk to me about it, Ryan. Journalists make choices."

His face reddened. "Want to talk about yesterday?"

"Nope."

I walked faster, and he didn't keep pace.

Mister Tibbs and I reached the edge of the bleachers, and she began to raise a leg. "Oops. Over here, girl."

We moved to a nearby tree. She pottied, fortunately not anything I'd have to pick up, and I poured some water into the paper cup. She lapped eagerly and raised a dripping face.

"You look so funny. Come on."

The bleachers were filling. Apparently the ones closest to the river were for fans of the military veterans.

Mister Tibbs and I strolled to the Chamber of Commerce side. We would root for both sides, but the Chamber and Rotary members were the people I'd bugged more for *South County News* stories, so I knew them better.

Members of the Chamber team were warming up, and a few more members walked by us. Mister Tibbs surprised me by giving a low growl.

Bruce Blackstone smiled and said, "Now Melanie, keep your wild dog under control."

"She smells my cat," Jagdish Patel said.

"You still have her?" I called.

"Can't get rid of her." He was a few feet past us and turned his head. "Want her? Or him."

Shirley's delighted laugh came from behind me. "Mel already has an androgynous dog."

She had changed from her Snack Shack apron to a ball player's striped shirt. Probably she'd already had on the sneakers, high cotton socks, and shorts, but I hadn't seen them when she was behind the counter. They looked incongruous with her teased hair.

As she reached me, I hissed, "I'm rooting for the Marines."

She laughed again. "Shug, everybody roots for the Marines."

The game could have been over in less than an hour, but it dragged on for nearly two. Brad Thomas hit a home run every time he was at bat for the veterans, often with people on base. Apparently, having him bat fourth was a strategic decision.

The Chamber team had a couple of strong players, but they also had people like Mr. Patel, who could be counted on to strike out or hit a pop fly every time at bat.

Shirley hit a line drive to the outfield, bases loaded, and three runs came in for the Chamber team. I think the military team member missed getting to the ball on purpose, so the score wouldn't be so lopsided.

During the seventh inning stretch, Mister Tibbs and I walked closer to the river. She had been lying under my legs, but I knew the noise was getting to her.

From my spot by the water, I noticed Nelson talking to a woman who held Rachel's hand. The woman, probably her mom, seemed to pass him something, but Nelson didn't have anything to give her.

I frowned. Should I do something? And what would that be? Tattle on a River's Edge resident and then testify in court if they were arrested for using illegal fireworks? I thought not.

Plus, even though I didn't plan to use them, I'd have to snitch on myself.

Harlan was not around, but over the next few minutes, despite raucous cheers from both sets of bleachers, Nelson moved through the crowd that stood along the sidelines. Because I knew what he sold, I was sure the nods were from people who agreed to buy or were told where to pick up their fireworks.

Maybe he did have a huge quantity to sell.

I was certain he was not the person who'd forced me into my closet. His voice wasn't all that distinctive, but I would have recognized even an effort to disguise it.

It hit me that I hadn't heard Harlan talk a lot. Could he have been my jailer?

When the game ended, fifteen to five in favor of the veterans, I didn't go back to the bleachers. Instead, Mister Tibbs and I walked along the river until we reached a place where it was easy to stroll up to Main Street.

"I don't know about you girl, but I wouldn't mind a nap before the fireworks.

She was so tired she didn't even yip.

CHAPTER NINETEEN

AFTER THAT NAP AND supper at the diner, I walked back to the park by the river. Getting there at seven-thirty would be plenty of time to watch kids play with sparklers and see who would win the adult potato sack race.

Judging from the insults being hurled about fifty yards behind me, the race hadn't started yet. Idly, I wondered why we still called it a potato sack race when plain burlap bags had been used for probably decades.

I hadn't brought a picnic basket, just a large jug of iced tea. Sandi had promised to bring some chips and salsa. Unspoken was that if she had learned more about Frost's death or my time in the closet, she would pass it on.

I spread a blanket on the ground, but didn't sit.

Maybe twenty yards out in the river, the company hired to conduct the fireworks had set up a portable, metal platform. River's Edge only buys one or two sky-high displays. They're too expensive. A lot of mid-sky fireworks still draw oohs and aahs.

The brisk air was thick with humidity, but not yet cool enough to be uncomfortable. That would come at dark, with more mosquitoes. Until then, my jeans would make me a bit warm, but at least I wouldn't need a ton of anti-itch meds in the morning.

Small tables rimmed the center of the park, boasting anything from homemade baked goods to embroidered flags to whittled flutes. Several of the latter were being played off-tune in various parts of the picnic area.

The Future Farmers of America had a display table describing its purpose. Whenever anyone got close to the four fresh-faced teens, they pointed to literature arrayed in front of them. Only adults stopped to talk.

I saw Brad and David's truck parked at the far end of the lot. The back end was raised. As people walked by it, they held their noses or fanned the air in front of their faces. Then they gave the truck a wide berth.

Though local people sold all kinds of things at the picnic area tables, most commercial vendors sold hot dogs, cotton candy, and small flags. In fact, I thought any commercial vendors had to be licensed. Why would Brad and David think they could sell manure at a Fourth of July fireworks event?

I deflected several sympathetic comments about Ambrose's arrest and kept scanning the area for Sandi. Finally she waved at me from near the Snack Shack, letting me know she'd join me in a minute.

The blanket I had placed on the grass had been mussed by people walking on it, so I straightened it. As I stood up again, I saw Brad lift a sack from the back of the truck and hand it to a guy in cutoffs and a red tee shirt. Brad, in a long-sleeved flannel shirt, was dressed for dirty work.

My first thought after *who would buy crap at a fireworks show* was that the mosquitoes were going to feast on the buyer's legs. My second was to wonder why he started to walk toward the field of picnickers.

Brad called something to him. The man laughed, turned, and started toward a nearby row of parked cars. His bag sagged in the middle, and I half-expected manure to spill on the parking lot. Or maybe it wouldn't because the bag sagged.

But a full bag of smelly manure wouldn't bend so much in the middle.

I remembered the woman who had argued with Brad and David at the Farmers' Market. She had wanted her bag delivered. It seemed like really poor service to make people carry their own... Their own...

Then it hit me. Fireworks! Brad and David didn't just sell stinky fertilizer. They were selling fireworks out of the back of the truck!

Except, wouldn't people notice? In bulk, fireworks smelled of black powder and sulfur.

But no one would smell fireworks in that truck because the scent of the bags of dung would cover any other odor.

I felt more excited than if I'd won the lottery. David and Brad were the competitors Nelson knew about. And their small panel truck would easily fit in our barn.

Two tow-headed boys about five years old ran in front of me, each holding a burning sparkler and laughing loudly.

A woman behind them yelled, "Mathew, Marcus! Stop running with those!"

The boys slowed to something close to a walk, still giggling.

My head turned toward the truck, and Brad met my gaze. I kept staring. Then I extended my arm and pointed at him. I lowered my arm and started walking toward the truck.

Brad must have realized my glower had nothing to do with fertilizer. He called something to David, but the latter was shaking a finger at two girls who had placed a conical firework about one foot high on the ground near the truck.

I focused on the girls. One was Rachel, whom I had earlier seen with her mom. She was wearing a tee-shirt with a cat on it, not unlike the one she'd petted when we met on the square.

The other girl was perhaps eleven or twelve, and I didn't know her. They didn't seem to like what David was saying to them.

Then I noted several other children by the truck. It seemed odd, until I remembered they probably knew Brad and David because their parents bought fireworks from the two men.

As I got closer, I realized the two girls planned to light their firework. The older girl bent over the yellow and orange cone.

"No," I whispered, and began to trot.

A flicker and sputtering red sparks said the firework had been lit. Rachel leaned close to it. That was stupid.

Where are her parents?

Brad had now jumped off the back of the truck and also yelled something at the girls.

A taller boy, maybe fifteen, had been about ten feet from Rachel. He turned to yell at Brad for hollering at Rachel. It was the older brother who had not seemed to like having Rachel trail him around the square. One of the two boys who raced kayaks earlier today.

Suddenly, Rachel shrieked and grabbed her hand. She tried to get her brother's attention by raising her probably stinging hand. He stood a few yards away, too busy yelling at Brad to notice.

Just sparks, it's only sparks.

I broke into a run. So did the older girl. She high-tailed it away from Rachel. Probably the girls weren't supposed to light the cones.

Other kids hurried away. They probably didn't want to get yelled at by Brad. Or their parents, who'd likely told the kids not to get near lit fireworks.

For some reason known only to him, Rachel's brother picked up the sputtering cone, which appeared about to go into full display, and pointed it at David, who ducked.

"Put the goddamned thing down," Brad yelled, but he didn't get close enough to try to grab it.

David stood up and leaned toward the boy.

The brother's red face had a contorted expression. With his back to Rachel, he dipped his arm. In an underhanded throw, he tossed the now sizzling cone at David.

David again demonstrated his ducking skills, and the cone, now spewing red and green sparks in a steady stream, landed in the truck.

Brad raised a fist and the brother, still seemingly unaware of Rachel, turned to run.

He thought he was throwing at a pile of dung. He doesn't know what he did.

I ran faster.

The yelling and Rachel's cries seemed to have aroused some attention. I thought I heard footfalls behind me. Probably a couple of parents running toward the truck.

David shouted, "Back away!"

Brad hollered, "Run!" And he did.

Rachel was rooted to her spot, crying ever more shrilly. Any adult at all close was rounding up their own kids.

I got to her, put one arm around her torso, and picked her up by the back waistband of her cotton pants with my other hand. I barely broke stride and ran like a gazelle, Rachel bouncing off my right hip.

We were only about twenty feet past the truck, when its fireworks began going off in earnest. Individually, they wouldn't have been too loud, but the percussion of the group bang inside a metal truck nearly pierced my eardrums.

Rachel kicked one foot. "Put me down! Mommy!"

Another twenty feet, and we reached the far edge of the picnic area, a good distance from the truck and not far from where I had placed my picnic blanket. I set Rachel on the ground.

She stopped screaming and reached behind her to pull her underwear out of her butt.

I glanced at her reddened hand. It surely stung, but wasn't a serious burn.

Rachel looked up at me. Both wide-eyed, we turned to watch a few of the exploding fireworks spew from the rear of the truck.

If I hadn't feared the potential explosion, the multiple colors and bright lights would have been fun to watch. I hoped against hope that the manure would block more from erupting from the panel truck. Or worse.

Screams and yells came from all around. A man's loud voice yelled, "It's terrorists!"

A bunch of people shouted him down. Probably people who had bought the illicit fireworks from David and Brad, I thought.

"We have to back up more," I commanded.

Rachel complied, staying next to me, now silent.

A man ran toward a Lincoln Navigator parked near the panel truck. He had keys in his hand.

"My God."

I had spoken softly, and Rachel asked, "Are you praying?"

The low rumble lasted only three or four seconds, just enough time for the Lincoln's owner to realize his life was more valuable than the car. He turned and sprinted far enough in two seconds to qualify for at least a state title, maybe the Olympics.

The explosion inside the truck thundered loudly, but it was the gas tank that added the sonic boom effect.

RACHEL'S PARENTS TOLD everyone within earshot that I'd saved their daughter's life. The term earshot wasn't really accurate, because I couldn't hear much of anything yet.

I kept backing away after each hug from her tearful mother.

Finally, Sandi rescued me by running up to say I had to help her with a story for the paper. She guided me by the elbow, with me walking backwards, until we were close to the Snack Shack.

My eyes stayed riveted on the remains of the now-smoldering chunks of metal that had been Brad and David's truck. The fire trucks had been on scene and used chemical flame retardant in addition to water. Any other night, they wouldn't have had as much of the retardant.

Because the two men had parked their truck toward the back of the lot, few cars had been near it. Even so, it looked as if the blast had shattered a lot of car windows. Shards of glass were everywhere.

Smoke had dissipated from the park, but the odor permeated my clothes and the air around us. It smelled like a cross between a bunch of stink bombs, a glowing fireplace, and an electrical fire. Kind of like when a toaster oven wouldn't turn off and the wires began to fray. But a lot worse.

People kept saying we were lucky no one got killed, but I hadn't seen David yet. I'd been too busy carting Rachel away from the truck to notice Brad and David when the explosion started.

"Melanie. Look at me!" Sandi's voice came through, dimly, and she sounded panicked.

I moved my gaze to her. "What?"

"Are you in shock? Are your ears okay?"

I touched my left ear. "The ringing's going down. Did you see David yet?"

"David Bates?"

I nodded toward the truck and back to Sandi. "It was his truck. His and Brad's."

Her eyes widened, and she looked toward the smoldering truck ruins. "I saw Brad."

We stared at the hunks of metal, saying nothing for almost a minute.

Aaron Granger's voice broke our reverie. "Uh, Melanie. Can you talk to me?"

He wasn't in uniform, but had his sheriff's deputy's badge pinned to a now-dirty tee shirt that had a picture of a burning firecracker and said, "Play safe."

I cleared my throat. "Sure."

"People said you grabbed the girl. Can you tell me how you happened to be close enough to do that?"

I whispered. "The truck. When I saw it tonight, I realized they used the fertilizer to cover the smell of the fireworks. They were selling fireworks."

His seemed more puzzled than anything. "So why go over there?"

My eyes filled with tears, and I looked at Granger more directly. "I think Brad and David were probably storing them in my barn."

His expression went from realization to horror, and he bent over and vomited into someone's open picnic basket.

CHAPTER TWENTY

SHERIFF GALLAGHER ASKED ME to come to the law enforcement building, but I took it as more of an order. He'd been annoyed that Sandi evaded him, but I told him she didn't know anything helpful.

When we got to the building, he put me at the table across from the desk in his office and left the door open. I think the dull tone of any responses I made had scared him.

Minus my purse with its pen and paper, I took a couple pages from the recycling tray near the sheriff's door and a pencil from his desk.

My notes were sloppy, a bulleted list even I could hardly read. But I wanted to write down every interaction I'd had with Brad and David in the last ten days.

When I saw the two men at the farmers' market, it hadn't seemed odd that Brad had inquired about Ambrose and me finding Peter Frost. A lot of people asked about Frost's murder right after we found his body. Hardly anybody asked after the sheriff arrested Ambrose for the murder.

Asking me how Frost had died, that was odd. Probably everyone in town knew he'd been stabbed. The *South County News* hadn't published by the Sunday of the farmer's market, but the story had been on local TV and in the *Des Moines Register*. Had Brad been trying to see what else I knew about Frost's death?

David had pulled up in front of Patel's store as I worked on the big pots for flowers. Kind of odd to drive the fertilizer truck around the square.

Why not just make his delivery somewhere and then switch to a car or pickup? Maybe he had recently dropped off fireworks orders. Or maybe it was his only transportation. Or had he been following me?

Get a grip. He probably drove around making deliveries.

I jotted down Nelson's name. He seemed to have known his competition. Maybe he could tell Sheriff Gallagher.

Something else, some other time I'd seen Brad and David, would not come to my mind.

Someone rapped lightly on the doorjamb. Aaron Granger, pale and drawn, stood there. "Can we talk?"

"Sure." I smiled slightly. "I'd invite you into my office, but it isn't mine."

That seemed to relax him. He walked around the table and sat across from me. "We talked to Brad."

"Did you find David?"

He looked away and then back to me. "In a manner of speaking."

"Oh, dear. He really died?"

His tone was cold. "I'm no medical examiner, but I'd say instantly."

I whispered. "And your uncle didn't die that way?"

"Sheriff'll have to talk more to you. I just...can't. I wanted to say I'm sorry."

I shook my head. "You saw Ambrose near your uncle with the knife."

He frowned. "More for what I said about you and Ambrose around town afterwards than the arrest itself."

I nodded, slowly. "Luckily it didn't get back to me. When you feel better, you can give Ambrose a call."

He stood. "I will." He walked out without saying anything else.

Saying Ambrose's name had been an important reminder. Even in Dubuque, he'd probably heard about the explosion. A news story might have even mentioned an unidentified body or missing people.

I took the new phone from the pocket of my jeans. I had given Ambrose the number, and the phone showed two missed calls – one from Ambrose and one from Sharon. My ears must have really been pounding to miss the phone's buzz.

I called him.

Ambrose opened with, "Sandi called and told me about the guys' truck blowing up and that you were safe. But she said you were with the sheriff." His tone hardened. "They trying to accuse *you* of something?"

"I'm glad she called. There's, uh, more, I think."

"What? Are you hurt?"

"No, just kind of flustered. It was, well, let's just say loud." I paused. "I mean I think they were using our barn."

"Who? Are you sure you're okay?"

"Brad Thomas and David Bates. I think they were storing fireworks in our barn."

Ambrose said nothing for maybe ten seconds. "Are you saying what I think you're saying?"

"I don't know for sure, but I think that's why I'm in Gallagher's office. I've heard, just maybe, they know you didn't kill Frost."

A dry sob came through the phone. I heard Sharon's alarmed cry. She must have been near him.

In a choked voice, Ambrose said, "No, it's okay. Mel's going to call back when she knows more." He hung up.

I stood up and walked to the water fountain in the hall. As I finished drinking, I saw Sheriff Gallagher at the end of the hall, talking to the fire chief. Gallagher had been in uniform tonight, and it bore sweat stains and black streaks.

He nodded toward his office. "I'll be down in a minute."

I didn't acknowledge him, but went back in and sat down.

A minute later he walked in, went behind his desk, and picked up the phone. Whoever he called didn't answer, because he left a terse message saying to call him back.

He looked at me. "I want to make sure the county attorney drops the charges against Ambrose first thing in the morning."

I shut my eyes for a couple of seconds and then looked at him. "Who did it? Brad or David?"

He sat down and snorted. "Brad says David, of course. I don't know how we would prove any different, but I asked Judge Morton for a warrant to search David's home and car. Might be something."

"And Brad's?"

"Yes. At the very least, we can get Brad for being an accomplice after the fact."

Gallagher paused. "I hadn't wanted to think Ambrose killed him, but between him holding the knife and Frost's body temperature, it sure looked like it."

I nodded, but didn't feel gracious enough to say I understood.

"What about fingerprints in our barn near the Velcro?"

Gallagher smiled. "You and your memory. But, no, they seem to have wiped down a lot of that barn. Probably didn't have to actually touch the building much, just the door."

"Did Brad say he used our house or locked me in the closet?"

"He acted as if he didn't even know there was a house on the property."

"There has to be a way… Hey, were there fingerprints on Mister Tibbs' collar?"

Sheriff Gallagher shook his head. "Only yours." He smiled. "Which, as you know, we had on file."

I didn't smile. "And, of course, he didn't have my phone."

"Correct. He has a lawyer. Right now, they aren't even volunteering to give us his fingerprints."

I brightened. "That says something, doesn't it?"

Gallagher shrugged. "Not really. Could just be the lawyer's advice, maybe he has a juvenile record he doesn't want me to see, though I don't know of anything. Brad's adult prints aren't on file."

I massaged the back of my neck and looked at Gallagher. "Too bad dogs can't do IDs in a lineup."

He grunted. "They might growl, but dogs growl at a lot…"

I nearly yelled. "What about a bite?"

"What about a bite?" he repeated.

"When some of the softball players walked by us in the park, Mister Tibbs growled. She never growls. Brad and David were with Bruce Blackstone and Jagdish Patel."

I talked too fast, and Gallagher looked as if he wanted to call a psychiatrist.

I took a breath. "If Brad or David took Mister Tibbs with them that day, why did they put her out of their truck?"

"Huh." Gallagher left the room without saying anything else.

I had thought something specific about Brad or David was eluding my memory. Instead, it was Mister Tibbs' growl at the softball field. I wished she were with me now.

After a minute, I stood and went to the doorway. I knew the room used to question people was not far from Gallagher's office.

After a few seconds, a man's voice, I assumed Brad's, yelled, "No way!"

The door to the nearby room was closed, so as voices lowered, I heard nothing more. I walked back to the chair I'd been using and sat, leaning forward to put my head on the sheriff's desk.

If Brad could be tied to Frost's death or, even if he couldn't but successfully blamed David, it would be over. Ambrose would be free, and the farm would be ours. I felt certain Aaron Granger would not continue his uncle's false claim.

I wanted to feel elated, but all I felt was cold and dizzy. Less dizzy than right after the explosion, but still light-headed.

The sheriff's office had no street-level window, but it did have a narrow window near the ceiling. From it came a mix of red and blue flashing lights, as well as a lot of bright white lights. I figured television trucks outside had set up portable lighting.

A door slammed nearby, and Sheriff Gallagher came back into his office.

I sat up and looked at him.

He smiled. "You'll be glad to know it looks as if the bite on his arm is getting infected."

I smiled weakly, as he walked behind his desk and faced me. "Did he admit Mister Tibbs made the bite?"

"No, but the county attorney will ask the judge to mandate a comparison." He frowned. "I'm sorry, but we'll probably have to have a vet do some kind of cast of Mister Tibbs' mouth. Doc Marshall can usually do that for us."

"Can she be asleep?"

He shrugged. "Not sure I can think of any other way a vet could do it." Seeing my expression, he added, "I bet we can arrange for you to be with your dog."

I nodded. "Now that you know Ambrose didn't do it, can you tell me anything more?"

Gallagher frowned lightly and said, "With the understanding that you won't repeat this to your reporter friends."

I snorted. "Not hardly."

He grunted. "It was a pretty one-sided article. All I'll say is the knife was one they were using to open boxes of fireworks. Brad says David reacted angrily to some demands Peter Frost was making."

I nodded. "I can believe it wasn't planned."

"Dead is dead," Gallagher said.

I certainly knew that. "Aaron came in."

He frowned lightly. "I asked him not to discuss it with you."

I smiled. "He actually didn't. He apologized for saying a bunch of stuff about Ambrose and me. You know, around town."

The sheriff's phone buzzed, and he picked it up. "Yeah? Okay. In a few."

He hung up. "Need to brief the media. Couple pictures of you hauling away little Rachel. People are calling you a hero. You want to talk to them?"

"No! Please, I don't want to."

He smiled fully. "I don't get off that easy. Hang on a bit, and I'll have someone drive you home. You can lie down in the car to avoid your media buddies."

At the word buddies I thought of Mister Tibbs. I needed a hug, but her slobber would do. It would do just fine.

CHAPTER TWENTY-ONE

THE DAY AFTER THE fireworks debacle, as the *Des Moines Register* had called it, I still had a lot of questions. I also had to spend time with Mister Tibbs, who had been frantic when I had gotten home. Too much noise, and I was absent from the apartment too long.

Mister Tibbs wandered into the kitchen, as I finished my second cup of coffee. She had been walking from room to room all morning, sitting or lying briefly and then resuming her patrol. At least that's how I thought of it.

"Come here, girl. You want to sit on my lap?"

Because I'd never said those words to her, she simply sat by the refrigerator and cocked her head at me. Perhaps she hoped for some of the leftover burger I occasionally brought home from the diner.

I stood from the table, walked to the living room, and sat in my recliner. I leaned back and patted my lap. Her ears perked up. She knew how to jump onto the recliner's foot rest. She made it in one quick leap.

"Come on, you can sit on me." I patted my lap again.

Walking slowly, as if she expected to be swatted to the floor, she reached my lap and sat.

"Ouch. Your nails are sharp. Lie down." I pressed on her middle gently, and she finally understood. In less than two seconds, her head was on my left shoulder and her belly faced me.

"There you go. See, you're safe."

I rubbed her head and then her belly. "Chill out, girl."

She relaxed into me and was sleeping in less than a minute. While she had become dead weight, her nap also gave me time to think.

The biggest disadvantage to being a gardener instead of a reporter was that I was out of the loop unless I inserted myself into a story or an investigation. I wanted to know so much.

Because, or as I'd heard before I left the sheriff last night, Brad Thomas admitted to something, there would be no immediate hearing as there had been for Ambrose. Plus, given the potential jeopardy David and Brad had put River's Edge residents in, it would be hard to argue Brad was not a danger to himself or others and should be out on bail.

I didn't know how Brad and David had gotten Ambrose's and my cell phone numbers to call us the day Frost died. They weren't our friends.

I supposed Frost had a phone with our numbers stored in it. He had called Ambrose and me a couple of times right after he filed suit. Then Ken Brownberg had told him to leave us alone and funnel all calls through Ken.

Unless it came out later, I didn't know whether Frost had been paid off to ignore our barn when fireworks were carted in or out. Surely someone would be looking into those cash deposits.

At Ambrose's hearing, we'd learned that Frost's call to Granger implied Frost was hurt or in trouble. What had he actually said?

Though Sheriff Gallagher would eventually be able to answer these and other questions if he wanted, a lot of what he learned would come from Aaron Granger. Would Granger talk to me?

I didn't want to call him at the law enforcement building, and I certainly didn't have his cell phone number. Stooper said Granger had been in Stooper's high school class, but given what Stooper had said about him, the two men weren't on good terms.

When in doubt about talking to anyone in River's Edge, the person to call was Shirley. She also collected phone numbers with the tidbits she treasured, so she might have Granger's. I shifted Mister Tibbs' weight and called her.

She didn't have his number. "But listen, Shug, he comes in for coffee if he works second shift. And it's Saturday. I think he's on that shift today."

Leave it to Shirley. I gave her my temporary cell phone number and hung up. Shirley would want to hear all about what Granger and I talked about, but she wouldn't blab about my request. She'd hold off for the bigger news later.

I tapped Mister Tibbs on the head. She opened her eyes, but quickly closed them. "Come on, girl, let's see if Stooper is at Dr. Carver's."

I'd said the magic word. She sprang off the recliner and walked to the door.

Like most vehicles that had been in the parking lot by the river last night, I had two broken windows. Luckily, the back of my truck had been pointed toward the direction of the explosion, so my front windshield hadn't blown out.

The back window had a huge crack, and the back seat windows were gone. I figured I'd drive to a dealer in Fairfield in a day or so. South County Glass probably had two-hundred work orders.

Rather than cover it with cardboard, I let Mister Tibbs ride with her head out the back seat window. I was spoiling her today, but I'd deal with the consequences later.

No Stooper at Dr. Carver's. Mister Tibbs and I got out anyway, and I called his cell.

"I'm working on a memorial stone for Peter Frost. Can't do garden stuff today."

"I didn't know you had that job."

"Granger called early today. I knew it was a cremated remains burial, didn't figure he'd want a big stone. And since you and me are buddies, I didn't think I'd get the work."

"Interesting." I thought for a moment. "Maybe it means he thinks it's all finally over."

"Could be. Gotta go."

I wondered if giving the work to Stooper was a deliberate sign of apology to me. Then I decided I was full of myself. Stooper probably charged less than any other mason, since he did the work at his home."

Mister Tibbs had spotted a squirrel she wanted to meet, but I ignored her squirming and pointed to my truck. "Come on, let's find Syl."

After the short drive from Dr. Carver's to Syl's place, I was disappointed that his truck wasn't in the driveway. What a letdown. I wasn't sure exactly why, other than I wanted someone to talk to and didn't feel like having it be anyone who wrote for the paper.

"Come on, Mister Tibbs. I'll water his plants some, and you can catch squirrels over here. Or run after them, anyway."

I had finished with the few vegetable plants behind the house and begun on the flower bed along the front when I noted an envelope taped to his front door. Even from twenty feet away, I could see MEL in large block letters.

I twisted the hose nozzle to off and retrieved the envelope. Syl's note said only, "You really stepped in it this time. Coffee tomorrow?"

I smiled. A good idea. I trudged to my truck for a pen and wrote, "Name the time." Then I stuck the note through his mail slot in his door. He didn't get his mail through the slot, but he'd see the note when he got inside.

While I watered the plants, I thought about Syl. He was in his early forties, which seemed too old for someone I'd date. But I definitely thought of him differently than

Stooper or Ryan. At least the way I thought about Ryan before he betrayed me with the biased story.

My cell phone vibrated, so I again turned the nozzle and placed the hose on the ground.

"Melanie here." Silence. "Hello?"

"It's Aaron Granger."

Shirley must have found him before his shift started. "I wasn't sure you'd call. Listen, can I buy you lunch at the diner?"

"That's probably more than I can handle, but I'll meet you for coffee. I don't start work until three."

I agreed to meet him at two and thought about his choice of words. I'd never thought of myself as hard to handle, though Sheriff Gallagher would. I figured Granger meant he couldn't talk about his uncle's death very easily.

I ARRIVED AT THE DINER at two, having had plenty of time to clean up and put on a pair of tan slacks and a yellow cotton shirt. I probably looked like a lemon, but I wasn't up for staid. I felt happy.

Granger was prompt. He nodded when he spotted me and walked toward the back booth that was always my preference.

Shirley got to the booth with two mugs of coffee before he had taken off his deputy's hat. "Decaf for you, Melanie, since it's afternoon. High test for you, Mister Sheriff's Deputy."

"Thanks," we both said.

I added cream, and he put in two packs of sugar but kept his black.

After fifteen seconds of silence, Granger asked, "What do you need, Melanie?"

"I wouldn't necessarily call it closure. I just can't figure out why Brad or David would hurt your uncle and then leave him in our barn. And then why call Ambrose and me?"

He took a deep breath. "First, they aren't too bright."

"They seem to have planned to incriminate us."

He shrugged. "Maybe, or maybe they simply wanted him found. I doubt they thought he would live long after they stabbed him."

I nodded. "I'm sorry it happened. Dr. MacGregor explained how someone stabbed where he was, um, could take a while to die."

"That will always be the hardest part for me."

When he said nothing more, I asked, "When did he call you?"

"About ten-thirty. My guess is that he was either unconscious for a time, or he waited until Bates and Thomas were out of the barn for good."

"And you told the judge you couldn't take the call?"

He nodded. "I was on the other side of the county. Burglary just past Fairhaven."

At the name of the place where Hal had stored his boat, our eyes met, and he looked away. "Anyway, you know how spotty service is. The call didn't ring, and it didn't show up in voice mail for, oh, maybe forty-five minutes."

"And he said he'd been hurt?" I asked.

"I wish he had. I would have sent an ambulance. His words were garbled. He said, 'I'm in Perkins' barn. I really pissed 'em off this time.' And then the call ended."

I took a sip of coffee. "That makes sense. You thought the 'them' meant Ambrose and me."

"I did."

We said nothing for another fifteen seconds or so. I would probably never fully know what Frost's call to his nephew meant, but I thought it meant he had been demanding money from Brad and David and had either gone too far or angered them badly in some other way.

I doubted whichever one stabbed him planned it. I could live with thinking it happened that way.

Finally, I said, "I wasn't fond of him, but I'm truly sorry you lost your uncle."

"Thanks. You probably want to know if I'm going to keep trying to get your farm."

I must have registered something like surprise, because he said, "No?"

"I suppose I figured you'd have no interest, but I didn't plan to ask you that."

"Well, I don't think… He'd been very poor, him and my mom, as kids. Then he bought the farm next to your parents, and the value went down. A lot."

I smiled. "Kind of hard to make that 'buy low, sell high' bit work all the time."

He grunted. "My guess is that he asked your dad about selling, and he said no. Uncle Peter maybe thought he would recoup his loss if he got your parents' place low. And he did have that yellow paper with the sketch. Then when your parents died…" He spread his hands in front of him as if to say he had finished speculating.

I had no comforting words. Peter Frost had put Ambrose and me through hell. I asked, "How's Bear?"

He sat up very straight and pointed at me. "I knew it. You were up there!"

I thought fast. He'd asked me if I'd seen a cat. He never said its name to me.

No lie would be plausible, so I said, "I was up there that night. I heard the meow. I wondered why no cat came up to me."

He frowned at me.

Thank God he didn't ask if I'd been in the house. "You have the cat?"

His expression cleared somewhat. "Yeah, I'll keep her." He took a big swig of his coffee.

I thought I'd try to catch him in a lie of omission. "What did you think of Hal's book?"

His expression could only be described as stony. "It's a bunch of crap. Uncle Peter would never..." He saw my smile and stopped. "Okay, I read it."

"Hal was a gas bag. If you don't think so, you're the only one in town."

"And he never liked Uncle Peter. He wouldn't subscribe to the paper when he moved to town."

"Hal's one-track mind," I murmured.

I had one more question and tried to sound casual. "Did you hear someone broke a window in my pickup one night, while it was parked outside Mrs. Keyser's?"

Granger raised his eyebrows. "No. Did you report it?"

I shook my head. "Ryan helped me tape it. Whoever it was scattered Hal's story all over the seat."

At first Granger's expression seemed puzzled, then he frowned. "Are you trying to say that I did...?"

I sat up straighter. "I just thought it was...odd. Why mess with Hal's story?"

He shrugged. "Probably didn't know it was a piece of crap."

I decided I believed him. Granger had already read the story when it was held in evidence. He could have made a copy. It made no sense for him to break into my truck. It must have been someone looking for easy cash.

Granger pushed his mug aside. "I'm all talked out Melanie. I am sorry you got dragged into this. You and Ambrose."

I smiled slightly. "I can see how it happened."

He began to reach into a pocket of his uniform, but I said, "My treat, remember?"

"I'm not sure I'll ever reciprocate."

I laughed. "I'm fine with that. Have fun with Bear."

His smile was the first genuine one I'd seen from Aaron Granger.

THE NEXT FEW DAYS WERE not easy, but at least people said they were glad about Ambrose or congratulated me for saving Rachel.

Scott Holmes had made that a big part of the July Fourth story. I took it as something of an apology, though I hadn't talked to him.

Syl and I shared an awkward cup of coffee. I really wished Stooper hadn't mentioned Andy's idea that Syl and I were having a fling. Unless we had something specific to talk about, I felt almost tongue-tied around Syl.

Mister Tibbs and I were getting into bed a couple of days later, when I opened the drawer to my bedside table and saw the manila folder with Hal's so-called mystery. I smiled ruefully, wondering how I could ever have taken it seriously.

As I shut the drawer, my eyes fell on the green scribble of my name, obviously in Hal's handwriting.

If the story wasn't about my parents, why was my name written across the top of the first page?

NOTE: Want more Melanie? The author suggests you start with her *From Newprint to Footprints*.

OTHER TITLES AVAILABLE
FROM
ANNIE ACORN PUBLISHING LLC

By Annie Acorn

Snowbound for Christmas and Other Stories
Luna Lake Cabins – The First Year
Christmas at the Cabins
Chocolate Can Kill
Murder With My Darling
The Magic Sand Dollar
A Tired Older Woman: Loses Weight and Keeps It Off!
Cover Design and YOU!
Pen & Ink 2014

Annie Acorn writing as Charlotte Kent

A Clue for Adrianna
A Man for Susan
Love's Journey
Love's Surprise
A Chester's Christmas
Love Blooms
A Christmas Kiss
A Valentine Surprise
Parisian Ghosts

By Angel Nichols

Cover Design and YOU!
The Ghost of Christmas Present and Other Stories
Thirteenth Door on the Left
A Rose by Any Other Name
The Christmas Thief
Storming the Friend Zone
To Catch a Grinch

By Juliette Hill

Pink Lemonade Diary
Finding Christmas Love
Christmas Shoppe Magic

By Andrea Twombly

Christmas at the Inn
Mildred Sauer's Christmas Gift

By Merrie Housdon

A Prince for Valentine's
A Chance with Destiny
A Maple Valley Christmas

By Susan Jean Ricci

My Sexy Chef
Chaos in the Kitchen

By Elaine Orr

From Newsprint to Footprints
Demise of a Devious Neighbor

By Peggy Teel writing as denise hays

Niki Knows the Dirt – A Niki Edgar Mystery
Monkey Business – A Niki Edgar Mystery

By Peggy Teel

God and Grandma

By Billie Thomas

Murder on the First Day of Christmas
Murder in a Two-Seater

Elaine L. Orr

Elaine L. Orr is the Amazon bestselling author of the nine-book Jolie Gentil cozy mystery series, set at the Jersey shore. *Behind the Walls* was a finalist for the 2014 Chanticleer Mystery and Mayhem Awards.

The first book in Elaine's River's Edge cozy mystery series, *From Newsprint to Footprints,* debuted in late fall 2015, with *Demise of a Devious Neighbor* to follow.

Elaine also writes plays and novellas, including the one-act, *Common Ground*, published in 2015. Her novella, *Biding Time,* was one of five finalists in the National Press Club's first fiction contest, in 1993.

Ms. Orr conducts presentations on electronic publishing and other writing-related topics. Nonfiction includes *Words to Write By: Getting Your Thoughts on Paper* and *Writing in Retirement: Putting New Year's Resolutions to Work*. A member of Sisters in Crime, Elaine grew up in Maryland and moved to the Midwest in 1994.

CPSIA information can be obtained
at www.ICGtesting.com
Printed in the USA
LVOW01s1603150317
527324LV00010B/936/P